*My lovely Lisa, the delightful Esme
and my incredibly supportive family.*

Thank you.

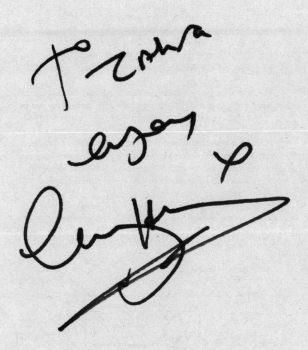

MACMILLAN CHILDREN'S BOOKS

Lenny Henry

Illustrated by Keenon Ferrell

THE BOY WITH WINGS

First published 2021 by Macmillan Children's Books

This edition published 2022 by Macmillan Children's Books
an imprint of Pan Macmillan
The Smithson, 6 Briset Street, London EC1M 5NR
EU representative: Macmillan Publishers Ireland Ltd, 1st Floor,
The Liffey Trust Centre, 117–126 Sheriff Street Upper
Dublin 1, D01 YC43
Associated companies throughout the world
www.panmacmillan.com

ISBN 978-1-5290-6784-2

1 3 5 7 9 8 6 4 2

A CIP catalogue record for this book is available from the British Library.

Printed and bound by CPI Group (UK) Ltd, Croydon CR0 4YY

Prologue

The magpie perched on the window ledge and peered through the glass, as if binge-watching its favourite television programme. The bird had abandoned its constant search for beetles, flies, caterpillars, spiders and worms (imagine that lot in a pie . . .). Right now, it just wanted to observe the boy.

The magpie had no idea why it wanted to watch the boy; it only knew that it was very, very important that it did. And so the busy-body bird stayed there on the sill, all the while keeping its shining dark eyes on him.

1

TUNDE IS TWELVE!

It was Tunde's twelfth birthday. He was having a party – a modest celebration with a few friends. He was looking forward to it and had no idea, not the slightest clue or faintest inkling, that it would end with a massive, knock-'em-down, fingers-up-the-nostrils, hair-pulling, nose-squishing BRAWL.

A few things to know about Tunde before we get going: Tunde was adopted.

He had no idea who his birth parents were or why they'd given him up. And he didn't much care either.

Well . . . that's what Tunde told his friends anyway. The truth about how he really felt about being adopted was BENDIER and **twistier** than a rubber band in a microwave.

Tunde's adopted mum and dad were called Ron and Ruth Wilkinson, and Tunde was very happy with them. They were cool.

For a start – they looked like him. They were dark skinned, Caribbean, but British born. They were hard-working, intelligent and loved him through and through. Tunde's mum, Ruth, was tall, had an epic Afro hairdo that she pulled back into a humongous bun (so big it could be seen from the moon, his dad would say) and gorgeous dark skin. She worked at a laboratory called **The Facility**, where she spent days staring at multiple screens, trying to get her computers to talk to each other. That was how she explained her job to Tunde, at least.

Ron Wilkinson was shorter than his wife. He had black curly hair, most of it on his head, but some **SPROUTED** from his ears and the neck of his shirt. He often joked about being part sheepdog. Ron also worked at The Facility, which is where he and Ruth had met. Ron's job involved taking fruit and veg and nuts and berries and seeds and, through scientific means, trying to make them bigger, stronger, more nutritious and tastier.

He enjoyed his work and often brought super-sized samples home with him. A marrow he'd winched through the window, the enormous blueberry that had to stay in the garden, the talking Atlantic salmon that lived in the bath for a while.

Tunde had never been inside The Facility but he had walked past it loads. It was famous in the neighbourhood. All the laboratories and testing grounds were surrounded by walls, fences and barbed wire, just like Scrooge McDuck's wallet.

Tunde got picked on a lot – at school, on the bus, even playing in the park – mostly because of the colour of his skin, so his mum and dad made sure to teach him about some of the great and successful people – inventors, explorers, athletes, doctors, nurses, scientists, and musicians – who looked exactly like him.

If anyone called him a horrible name at school, they told Tunde to think of:

- Benjamin Banneker, an inventor who'd made a clock that kept perfect time for forty years.
- Muhammad Ali, who'd won the boxing heavyweight world championship three times in a row.
- Dr Martin Luther King, Jr., who'd marched and braved high-powered water hoses and vicious dogs in order to gain freedom for people who looked like Tunde.
- And . . . Garrett Morgan, the bloke who invented the traffic light.

Tunde remembered them all, but he still found it difficult not to cry when he was picked on by name-calling hooligans with fewer brain cells than a potato.

Knowing the name and achievements of a boxer doesn't mean you can beat the biggest bully in your year in a fight (at Tunde's school this was Quinn Patterson). It just means you've got a good memory.

Whenever Tunde tried to explain this to his dad, Ron would say, 'Son, there's a time when you have to stand up for what's right. Sometimes the only way to deal with a bully is to bonk 'em once, hard on the beezer. That'll teach 'em a lesson.'

Then he'd cackle like a mad wizard, point to his nose, **SQUIDGE** it and go, 'HONK HONK!'

Tunde didn't want to bonk anybody on the beezer, partly

because he wasn't that keen on violence and partly because he didn't want to get into trouble. Still, he appreciated the advice.

Sometimes his dad would try and cheer him up with a terrible joke. For instance, if Tunde felt sad, Ron would scratch his head, hitch up his pants and say:

Knock, knock.
Who's there?
Candice.
Candice who?
Candice door open soon, I'm dyin' for a wee!

There were more where that came from; some of Ron's other favourite jokes included:

Why did the apple turnover?
Because he couldn't get to sleep.

Or:

What did the mummy tomato say to the baby tomato that was lagging behind?
Ketchup!

Tunde never found them quite as funny as his dad did, but seeing him roar with laughter at his own jokes made Tunde happy.

The truth was, Tunde got on well with his mum and dad.

His life, aside from Quinn Patterson and his gang of smelly yobboes, was good.

Even so, sometimes those TWISTY, melty, rubber-band-in-a-microwave feelings about being adopted would niggle away at him and he'd have to push them down inside. Anyway, back to Tunde's twelfth birthday, and the party that would end in a massive brawl that would make even Muhammad Ali proud.

Party day began bright and sunny. Tunde's mum had gone to **LOADS** of effort – frying, baking, steaming, slicing, dicing. As usual, there was WAY TOO MUCH food and, knowing Tunde's mum's cooking, quite a bit of it would be inedible.

Tunde had invited his best friends from school: Kylie Collins, Jiah Patel and Nev Carter. Just three guests. They could all fit into a shoebox if pushed.

Kylie Collins rocked a wheelchair, had perfect aim with a bow and arrow, and her mum was a relationship counsellor. Kylie often repeated things she'd heard her mum say at work, such as: 'Don't just say how you feel: show it!'

And:

'The height of madness is doing the same thing over and over and expecting a different result.'

And, best of all:

'If you're going to fight, fight productively!'

Jiah Patel, who was very practical, thought this last one was particularly high-larious. 'Brilliant, so if I'm being pummelled by maniac zombies, I should build a Lego model of Disney World? Productivity in action!'

Jiah was a mathlete. She didn't care what anyone thought about her . . . apart from her parents, that is. As far as they were concerned, school was one big, bloodthirsty, no-holds-barred competition and if you weren't in it, no way could you win it.

Jiah wore glasses, had read every comic book ever, sometimes went on a bit, and was the kindest person they knew. Even so, Kylie and Tunde were no longer shy about telling her to put a sock in it.

Then, there was the **GUEST OF HONOUR**, the Coolest Guy in the School (perhaps the entire universe!) in Tunde's eyes: Nev Carter!

Nev was fit as a flea; the kind of flea that works out three times a day and does yoga at the weekend. They hadn't been friends that long, but they'd hit it off big-time. Tunde had been praying feverishly that Nev would attend the party. He didn't want to be the only boy there. That would be **MAJOR LEAGUE AWKWARD**. Tunde would then be crowned the King of Awk-land. He shuddered at the thought.

Tunde helped his parents set out the various party foods on a trestle table by the kitchen door, then excitedly waited for the guests to arrive.

Kylie got there first. Her taxi screeched to a halt by the front gate and, once she'd told the driver off for speeding, she zipped into the garden.

'Whoa! Tunde, your garden's **giNORmous!** You could land two 747s sideways in that allotment, I'm not even jokin'!' She wasn't wrong. The Wilkinsons had a vast lawn, an orchard of fruit trees, and a picture-perfect allotment. The garden, with its clever and precise landscaping, was entirely down to Tunde's dad's new-found obsession with gardening.

It had all started when he'd been passed over for promotion **yet again**. The powers that be just didn't think super-sized, super-tasty fruit and veg were that important.

Ron told everyone that he didn't mind being overlooked yet again, even though his face told a different story – but shortly afterwards, he started doing a lot of gardening.

In the last year, Ron had spent nearly all his spare time mowing, trimming, cutting and strimming, clipping, pruning, planting, fine-tuning, raking, hoeing, composting and sowing.

The garden used to be completely wild, so bad Amazon explorers would have given up at the front gate. Tunde had overheard his mum a gazillion times saying things like:

'Well, I'd like to go out and hang the washing, but I'd need a map and a massive machete to get there.' Or she might say:

'Ron, I'm heading to bed – and, just for a change, I won't use the stairs. I'll use the fifty foot of ivy that's growing through the cracks in our walls . . .'

So, when Ron started organizing the garden in an obsessive way, Ruth was thrilled. At first. However, after a while, this mania had become . . . a bit much. Both Tunde and his mum hoped Dad would finally get a promotion at The Facility. Then maybe he would stop trimming the hedge with nail scissors.

Now, as Kylie **whizzed** up and down the garden's various, neatly mapped pathways exclaiming, 'Dude, did your dad do all this with a big ruler?' Nev and Jiah arrived, bearing gifts.

Although this was his twelfth birthday, an age when a lot of kids turn their backs on childish things like Father Christmas, the Easter Bunny and things like that, Tunde loved getting presents! He tore the Sellotape off with his teeth, just to get a look at his swag.

Nev had bought him a Manchester City sweatshirt. Tunde blinked rapidly, several times, as he stared at it. He supported Liverpool FC – surely Nev knew that? They'd talked a huge amount about football. He blinked several more times, unsure of what to say. If he was Superman, this shirt would be Kryptonite. He was speechless and just stood there, stunned.

Nev laughed out loud. 'Mate, I know you're Liverpool, but I thought I'd buy you this. So you know what real class looks like!'

He tried to wrestle the top over Tunde's head. 'Nooooooooooo!' Tunde yelled and *ducked* and **DODGED** to get free from the clearly contagious shirt.

Nev laughed. 'Are you running away from me now? Well, you won't be wanting this then!'

And from behind his back, he produced a **humongous** Chocolate Orange. Tunde was impressed – he loved Chocolate Oranges and this one was bigger than his entire head. Of course Nev would bring the coolest presents. He couldn't stop smiling.

'Open mine next,' said Jiah, proudly plonking a package on the trestle table. Tunde squeezed it a couple of times to see if he could guess what was inside – it felt soft. In the end, intrigued, he ripped the package open to reveal several pairs of multicoloured socks. Boring! He tried to fake a smile, though could only manage a four out of ten, tops, and said:

'Thanks, Jiah! Socks! They're great!'

Jiah rolled her eyes. 'You need to look!'

Tunde did, and saw that the socks were carefully embroidered with . . . arithmetic problems. The label on the footwear said MATHSOX.

Tunde suppressed a scream of alarm. Why would anyone think this was a good idea? He imagined himself, last thing at night, taking his shoes off to reveal his feet covered in complex maths problems. He shook his head to lose the image. Maybe he'd hide them under the mattress until . . . the end of time.

'Thanks, I love them,' he said, hiding his insincerity as best he could.

Jiah beamed.

'I knew you would,' she said modestly.

Inside, he breathed a sigh of relief – he should get, at least, an Oscar, a BAFTA or another giant Chocolate Orange for that performance. Mathsox? **YIKES**.

Finally, Kylie handed him an envelope which, once opened, revealed a £20 music voucher.

'Thanks, Kylie,' Tunde said. 'This is genuinely useful.' He loved listening to music. Nev was teaching him all about Grime, Drill, House, Hip-hop, Hip House, Trap-House – basically anything that would confuse the heck out of his mum and dad.

Tunde looked around at his small group of friends; his

heart was full. They were awesome. It had taken ages for them to find each other.

Before these guys he had made a big effort to make friends at school – but had failed miserably. He just didn't seem to fit in anywhere.

His beaky nose made him stick out from the other kids of colour, and his jet-black skin and curly hair meant that a lot of the white kids (and there were mostly white kids at his school) didn't want anything to do with him. He felt like a stone in somebody's shoe. Unwanted, annoying, and difficult to deal with.

But then, a year ago, Tunde had found his tribe. He and Kylie had both started laughing at their form teacher's hairy nostrils one morning (one hair stuck out at least two feet! If he sneezed Kylie imagined it cracking like a whip!) and they had both been told off. Every time they had looked at each other that morning, they had burst out laughing again.

At break, Kylie had introduced Tunde to Jiah (who immediately handed him two comic books, told him three jokes and informed him that he'd got four of the last maths homework questions wrong) and from that moment on, they'd had each other's backs, whilst everyone else threw mud, paint, or the contents of their lunch boxes at them.

Let's face it – school is hell if you're any kind of nerd; and if you happen to look like Tunde, it's probably even worse. You might find yourself practically swarming in enemies or bullies or both.

Speaking of which, we present:

EXHIBIT A: Quinn Patterson. One of seven brothers – all with a bad attitude. He was already famous at school for being the kind of kid you wouldn't want to meet down a dark alley. In fact, a dark alley had recently written an online article with the heading: 'Quinn Patterson gives us a bad name'.

Quinn was the self-declared emperor of a rag-tag, nose-picking, flatulent crew consisting of his faithful number two, Sanjay Khan, tough Billy Willis, and the enormous (for his age) Pauly Gore.

This lot were notorious for (a) Not being that bright; and (b) Their fierce loyalty to Quinn. Whatever he asked of them, they would do, whether it was to:

- Jump off a cliff.
- Eat their own bogeys with a knife and fork.
- Roll around in grass without checking for dog poo first.
- Give nerds upside-down swirlies in the toilets.
- Shove chewing gum in some poor girl's hair.
- Make bubbly, squelchy, fart-type noises in class.

The gang were a **total menace**. Their only mission in life was to make Quinn laugh so hard he'd squirt lemonade from both nostrils. Double-barrelled Nose-hole Blast! Ugh.

Because Quinn made fun of Tunde all day, every day at school, he was positively, definitely, absolutely with big giant bells on – the last person on Earth that Tunde would invite to his birthday party.

Which is why it was such a surprise when, just as Tunde

had finished unwrapping most of his presents, Quinn and his crew arrived by the back gate.

Tunde, Kylie, Jiah and Nev stared in horror as this delegation of dorks pulled up on their battered bikes, like cash-strapped Hell's Angels who were saving up for real motorbikes soon. After watching them for a while, Tunde made a decision. 'Let's just ignore them,' he whispered. 'We can't let them spoil the fun.'

Jiah, however, had to be restrained.

'I'm going to give them a large piece of my mind,' she said, adopting a complicated kung-fu stance she'd recently learned from a martial-arts-superhero-time-travel film, even though she knew nothing about martial arts, wasn't a superhero and had never, as far as they knew, time-travelled.

'Just chill, fam,' Nev said. 'Don't even look at them, let's just enjoy ourselves.'

But Quinn could sense the fear in the air. He grinned like an unhinged hyena circling its prey as he wheeled back and forth and forth and back, his wicked smile visible just above the garden wall, his cronies hanging on his every word.

'Hey,' said Quinn loudly. 'What's the word for a group of nerds? What about "a vomit of nerds?"'

They cracked up. Pauly laughed so hard he fell off his bike, which was too small for him anyway.

Sanjay jumped in with:

'Nah, nah, nah, it's a bogey of nerds, innit?'

This got a few laughs, but not as many as Quinn's attempt. Billy thought with all his might. You could almost hear the machinery in his brain churning, like a rusted steam-engine being coaxed to life.

'A skidmark of nerds. Like in your pants at bedtime!' An explosion of snorts and cackles followed this, making Billy momentarily feel like the king of the castle.

Tunde sighed. It was going to be a long afternoon. Tunde's mum came over. 'Why don't your other friends come in, luv?' she said, catching sight of Quinn's gang. 'They can't just sit around on their bikes outside. Those seats don't look comfortable and they'll just get sore bottoms and then you'll feel guilty.' Kylie and Jiah laughed.

'Mrs Wilkinson, these dungheads are most definitely not our friends! In fact, they're our sworn enemies!' declared Kylie.

Ruth frowned. 'Enemies is a strong word, Kylie. Maybe they just want to be included,' she said. 'Maybe they secretly want to be friends!'

Tunde was thinking that he'd rather be friends with a Cape buffalo with bad breath, but he kept that to himself and just said:

'Believe me, they don't.'

His mum sighed. 'Oh well. Just keep trying. Now, how about some birthday cake? I think you're going to love it.' Tunde wasn't so sure. His mother's experimental baking teetered on the boundaries of edible. She wouldn't make it past the auditions for *Bake Off*, let alone the first week. He and his dad never knew whether to eat it or drop it from the roof to see if it bounced.

Tunde's mum dashed back into the house, returning

seconds later with Dad in tow, proudly bearing a large, red, gold, green and white cake.

It was book-shaped and Tunde recognized the design immediately. It was based on the book *The Real McCoy*, and it was about inventors, explorers, politicians, musicians, doctors, athletes, in fact anyone who had made a big difference in people's lives and looked like Tunde.

Tunde walked over to the cake and looked at all the little figures carved from marzipan:

- There was the le-gend-ary, G-O-A-T gymnast.
- There were the famous women mathematicians who'd helped send rockets into space.
- There was the footballer who helped with the free school meals for kids.

And there was – hang on. What was that extremely handsome dude from that cop show that Mum had a crush on doing there, shaped from marzipan like a Roman statue?

Ron muttered, 'Why is he on there?' and Ruth shushed him, saying, 'Because he's gorgeous . . . and he looks like Tunde, that's why.'

There was a small figure at the centre of the cake – a little brown boy with a longish, pointy-ish nose and the words **HAPPY BIRTHDAY TO OUR BEAUTIFUL BOY** just underneath.

Tunde blushed with embarrassment.

His mum cut a portion of cake. Tunde peered at it and

recoiled as he saw nuts, berries, seeds, beetroot, sponge mix, cream, and some type of weird greenish jam.

Tunde looked at his mum. 'I'm not sure that's really a cake, Mum,' he said. 'It's raw – it might be alive . . . parts of it are moving. It looks like something's breathing in there!'

Even Dad laughed at that; Nev, Jiah and Kylie were having to turn away as they were giggling so much.

Ruth glared at Tunde for a moment, placed the mutant cake on the trestle table, and nodded to Ron, who went back inside the house and returned seconds later with a platter of doughnuts, chocolate eclairs and a shop-bought trifle.

Ruth looked a bit sad. 'I know not everyone likes my baking, but it's all made with love, Tunde, and that's what matters the most. Besides, I happen to like raw cake. But you can all eat the boring, ordinary cakes if you want . . .'

'Well done, Ruth,' said Ron, patting her on the back, 'it looks spectacular-licious.' He smiled. 'Now, come on, peeps – charge your paper cups with more orange squash and let's drink a brill-tissimo-tastic toast to our lovely son and your friend – Tunde!'

Ron poured way too much sugar-free squash into plastic cups for everyone and they all sang 'For He's a Jolly Good Fellow' and 'Happy Birthday, Dear Tunde' and then cheered.

And then Ruth announced that she and Ron would disappear for a couple of hours, 'While you enjoy yourselves. But if we're all to remain friends – you know the rules.'

Tunde's mum and dad were keen on rules, so that things didn't get 'Out Of Hand'.

The Rules were:

- Clean up after yourselves.
- Be respectful.
- Do not mess with the garden. Repeat: do not mess with the garden.
- If you're playing music, level six should be more than adequate.

'Happy birthday, Tunde,' his mum said. 'And don't forget, we haven't given you your special present yet! We'll do it when we get back from the shops. You kids have fun.' She said that bit in a fake American accent that made Ron laugh.

Tunde watched as they got into the car and drove off, waving 'til they were out of sight.

Nev laughed. 'Mate, I'm not being funny, but your mum should NEVER go on *Bake Off*. Some of them little figures look well wonky, innit?'

Kylie came to Tunde's defence. 'C'mon, you lot, parents are off limits!'

Tunde just laughed, shook his head, looked at all the food and yelled out:

'All right, shall we get this party started or what?' They all went WOOHOO! And whilst skilfully avoiding the **RADIOACTIVE** seeds-nuts-mutant-weirdo cake, began feasting with gusto on tuna, chicken, ham, and egg mayonnaise sandwiches, hummus and pita bread, chicken nuggets, pizza slices, chocolate eclairs and trifle. Kylie was a touch overwhelmed by the amount of food that had been laid on.

'Tunde! There's enough food here to feed the entire school AND the cast of *The Lion King*.'

Tunde nodded. He hadn't had the heart to tell his parents that only three people were coming. He didn't want them to think he was a total loser.

They ate until they'd had their fill and said things like, 'I can't move. I've had fourteen chicken sandwiches, and they're all stuck here just above my belly button' and, 'I could eat pizza slices like this for breakfast, dinner and tea, bruv,' and, 'I know this is weird, but you've got to try a chocolate eclair with hummus and ham on the pita bread – it's gonna change your life, trust me!'

Once they'd thoroughly discussed the effect this variety of sweet and savoury foods was having on their insides – they decided to play some party games.

Kylie had made an exhaustive list of all her favourite ones. Meanwhile, Nev had hooked his phone up to the speakers and pumped out his latest playlist. Jiah, with great ceremony, produced a stack of papers from her rucksack and handed them to Tunde with a flourish.

'It's a birthday quiz,' she explained.

Tunde gingerly looked through the document. 'Jiah, this is thirty pages long.' He flipped through the pages and added, 'And I don't understand any of it!' Jiah's quiz contained a series of DEVILISHLY DIFFICULT maths problems, including a dizzying array of graphs, sums and equations, as well as questions about time and space and quantum physics.

Tunde patted Jiah on the shoulder. 'I'm gonna set fire to this, OK?'

Everybody except Jiah cheered.

'Maths is fun!' she said. 'If you get good enough, you could end up running the country, Mum says.'

Kylie pretended to throw up. Nev wasn't really listening as he was busy doing a handstand and bouncing a ball off his feet.

Tunde said, 'Sorry, Jiah. Nobody wants to do maths at a party!'

Jiah shrugged. 'Your loss! What do you want to do then?' Nev did a backflip, landed upright again and said, 'Leave this to me,' and the games began.

First there was a legendary three-legged-one-leg-and-two-wheels race: Tunde and Nev versus Kylie and Jiah. Nev thought it was cheating when Jiah basically got a lift from Kylie and, using the electric assist on her chair, zoomed to the finish line, screaming in victory: 'We rule! C'mon, best of three!'

Then Jiah, Nev and Tunde attempted to walk on their hands while Kylie commentated as if on TV:

'Welcome to the inaugural hand sprint at the Wilkinson stadium. Carter, Patel and Wilkinson are neck-and-neck. The crowd are beside themselves with joy as Wilkinson takes the lead! But, my goodness, here comes Carter — it's as if he's walking on his feet — gathering momentum! Wait! Wilkinson puts on a spurt of speed and . . . oh my word!'

Which was when Jiah slipped on a rotten apple and freaked out, wailing, 'It's dog doo-doo, it's dog doo-doo! I need hand sanitizer NOW!'

She promptly bumped into Tunde and Nev, who collapsed almost head first into a mini compost heap. Kylie roared with laughter.

'This is extraordinary! Wilkinson and Carter have just narrowly escaped being plastered in household waste – it's a **POO-TASTROPHE!** My goodness!'

And then, just as they were all having loads of fun, everything changed.

They'd managed to forget all about the gang of jealous thugs watching from outside the gate. But suddenly, there they were, clambering over the garden wall, like fun-sized

Vikings: Quinn Patterson, Sanjay, Billy and Pauly. Quinn's face was a lurid portrait of barely suppressed contempt.

'Nice party. How come yer never invited us, Beaky? We not good enough for ya?'

The other boys lumbered up to the trestle table and grabbed handfuls of cake, pocketed sweets and drank squash straight from the jug. Pauly Gore took a mouthful, swirled it round for a moment and then spat back into the jug. 'For extra flavour!' he leered, much to his mates' amusement.

Nev had seen enough 'Quinn, you ain't welcome, man. Your name's not down. Bog off home.'

Quinn's crew formed a protective wall in front of him as he stepped forward.

'I can go anywhere I want, Nev. You're not my dad!' Tunde instinctively looked around for his parents but, of course, they were nowhere to be seen.

Jiah piped up, bold as brass. 'No, we've all seen your dad at Sports Day, Quinn. You need to tell him that technically, that's not how you water a rose bush!'

Nev and Kylie laughed, despite their nerves. Jiah folded her arms. Quinn's jaw clenched. He wasn't used to nerds standing up to him, however nerdily they did it, and his blood was up. He wanted a fight.

Tunde took a deep breath and then heard himself say, 'You lot need to leave right now – so get lost!'

His heart froze. He couldn't believe he'd said that. Why did he say that? Was he . . . getting braver?

Quinn drank and then snorted squash from his flared

nostrils and rounded on Tunde, his hideous hyena grin taking pride of place right there smack in the middle of his mush.

'Who d'ya think you are, Beak-o? The King of England? So what if I didn't get a silly little card with gold writing on it, inviting me to your silly party? I don't need your permission to go anywhere!'

'I invited my mates. Not you,' Tunde shot back.

Sanjay interrupted, 'Ha! You call four nerdy losers stuffing **boring** cake into their **boring** faces a party? Nice try, Beakzilla!'

Kylie screeched up to them, her face bright red. She brandished her phone. 'Get out or I'm calling Tunde's mum and dad.'

Gore giggled, pushed the joystick back on Kylie's chair, and she reversed towards a nearby, recently trimmed, very bulbous hedge. Nev ran after her, but she'd already stopped her chair before she became further embedded in foliage.

'That's ENOUGH!' yelled Tunde. 'You're NOT gonna push us around ANY MORE.'

Quinn gave a nasty leer. 'That's where you're wrong, Beak-o-saurus!'

He clicked his fingers, and Sanjay and Billy ran up to the trestle table and overturned it. Billy tap-danced in the ruins of the cake and **smeared** it into the grass.

Sanjay upended two spare jugs of squash on to the paved path. Pauly grabbed hold of Nev by the neck and thumped him in the face (Tunde would've helped but the blood made him think twice).

Jiah screamed and lashed out at Billy as he egged Pauly on. Kylie was very frustrated by now as she'd almost taken root in the giant hedge.

'Hang on,' said Quinn, his eyes alight with curiosity. 'What's that?'

Quinn approached what looked like a gift-wrapped bicycle (which is exactly what it was) propped against the side wall of the house. Tunde raced after him, his heart sinking. This was his special present from Mum and Dad.

'Wait, leave that alone.' His voice sounded fearful, feeble and weak. Why did this have to happen today?

Quinn Patterson mocked him, tore at the wrapping paper and simpered: 'Ooh, is this yer **big important** present? I know: Why don't I open it for you? I bet it's rubbish!'

The gang watched in silence as he ripped away at the garish wrapping paper until the bike underneath was revealed. Granted, it was second-hand, but it had been fixed up and was as good as new – with a brand-new seat, tyres, reflectors and an impressive metallic-blue paint job.

Quinn was impressed. 'Wow. This's actually awesome, Beak-Bonce . . . better than mine. You know what, lads? I'm having it.' And he wheeled Tunde's new bike towards the garden gate.

Now, there are times in life when enough is enough. Some call this moment 'The Tipping Point'. Some say it's 'The Straw That Broke the Camel's Back' (Tunde never understood that saying. Whose camel was it? How much straw does it take to break a camel's back? A ton? A kiloton? A gazilo-ton? He had so many questions.)

This was Tunde's tipping point. He'd had just about enough of Patterson's shenanigans. He looked around at his friends. Jiah was trying not to cry. Nev was trying to stop his nose bleeding by tilting his head up. Kylie was yelling that she was calling the police NOW!

Tunde shook with anger. His party had been wrecked,

ruined and ransacked. His voice cracked with rage. 'Put my bike back and get out.'

Quinn just ignored him and carelessly chucked the birthday bike over the garden wall. Tunde's precious gift clattered against the other bikes and then tumbled, handlebars first, into the road: it looked like an upended stag.

Tunde kicked the base of the ancient apple tree, which stood centurion-like by the garden wall, and let out an **IMPASSIONED SCREAM**. (Later, Nev, Jiah and Kylie would say this desperate cry was the weirdest sound they'd ever heard coming from a fellow human being.)

Quinn turned, surprised despite himself, and laughed. 'What you **squawking** about, yer big baby? It's only second-hand. Your mum and dad shoulda worked harder an' got you a new one!'

But Tunde was no longer looking at Quinn. His attention was somewhere else.

A single magpie had landed on a low-hanging branch of the apple tree, cocked its head and locked eyes with Tunde. Tunde stared back, tears coursing down his face. 'Come on,' Quinn yelled. 'Let's go, this party's proper rubbish!' With that, he and his cronies jumped over the wall, laughing.

Dropping on to the other side, Quinn picked up Tunde's bike and, smirking with glee, shouted, 'Wave buh-bye to your birthday bike, Beaky!'

But Tunde wasn't listening – the magpies were multiplying!

There were three magpies now, then twelve, then ninety-six. Suddenly the entire tree sagged under the weight of this rogue mega-gulp of magpies.

There were hundreds of them.

'I don't like the look of this,' said Nev, peering at the birds. 'Tunde, birds are scary smart, fam. I'm off inside. Let's leg it, yeah?'

Kylie, Jiah and Nev retreated, wide-eyed and frightened, towards the house. But, somehow, Tunde wasn't scared. He was emotional, though; very, very emotional.

'I HATE that lot!' he screamed.

And, as if on cue, the magpies rose into the air in an eruption of beaks, claws and feathers.

Quinn and his gang were oblivious to this meteoric massing of magpies. The boys ambled away from the house, wheeling their bikes beside them and sniggering at what they'd done.

Pauly bragged. Billy gloated. Sanjay laughed. Meanwhile, Quinn was inspecting Tunde's two-wheeled birthday present for marks and scratches.

'This bike ent bad y'know? First day back at school when I ride this in – it's gonna really get up El-Beako's stupid nose. D'you see him crying?'

He mimicked Tunde's distress. 'That's myyyyyy bike, nyerr nyerr nyerrrr! You leave my bike alone, bleh bleh bleh! I want my mummy! Honestly? I thought he was gonna do one in his nappy!'

The cronies laughed it up as usual.

But then, one by one, their laughter died as they turned away from him.

Quinn looked at them, puzzled; he was used to his devoted,

captive and not very bright audience hanging onto his every word as usual. He noticed they were all looking up, so he did too.

'Wh-what is that?' he gasped.

And with that he dropped the stolen bike with a loud CLANG and sprinted off down the road, followed by a totally terrified trio.

They were right to be scared; bearing down on them were

what looked like a ferocious blur of over a thousand magpies, soaring at almost supersonic speed.

Within seconds they enshrouded the gang, squawking, screeching, croaking, crowing, calling and crying for who they got to peck first. The screams of Quinn, Billy, Pauly and Sanjay could be heard all the way back at Tunde's house.

Just in time, the bus arrived. They pulled their jackets over their heads and ran to get on. Quinn yelled: 'Driver, shut the door NOW! Go, go, go, go, go!'

The bus driver almost lost his grip on the wheel as he saw the legion of magpies **WHOOSHING** towards them. He stomped his foot down on the accelerator and the bus lurched off.

Inside, the scene was utter pandemonium. The other passengers gawped in alarm and confusion as Quinn and his gang ran back and forth like hysterical, wobbly-legged, headless turkeys, slamming all the windows shut as magpies scrabbled and scratched at the glass. At last, Quinn managed to bang the last window shut, causing a few of the birds to plummet to the ground in the process. **THUMP! BUMP! Ka-WHUMP!**

The dazed birds took wing immediately, relatively unscathed. Quinn slumped down breathless in his seat and Billy, Pauly and Sanjay – all wild-eyed and breathing heavily – joined him.

They took stock of their injuries. Pauly had received a mass of red dots all over his head and hands.

Sanjay bore nasty scratches on his arms. Billy's ear was

bleeding. Quinn had been slashed on the arm, shoulder, and back of the neck. He sat quietly and tried to work out what had just happened.

'That was horrible,' he whispered. 'Like one of them horror movies.'

'Yeah,' said Pauly, wiping sweat from his forehead. 'I thought that was it! We're lucky to be alive.' Sanjay told him to stop being 'such a dramatic nurk'; Billy was busy trying not to cry.

If they'd all turned to glance through the back window, they would have seen Tunde retrieve his newish bike, and walk back towards the house. They would also have seen him stop and stare at the magpies overhead, puzzled. They would have witnessed that huge conglomeration of birds explode outward and disperse in all directions.

②
A MURMURATION

The Magpie Incident wasn't the first time Tunde had experienced an intervention from things with wings. Back in junior school, for instance, Tunde had really wanted to make friends with . . . anyone, really. He wanted to run and jump in puddles and fall off the rickety rides in the extremely life-threatening adventure playground, but his classmates (some of them anyway) were put off by his appearance. They said things like:

> Tunde's well brown, innit?
> And his hair's too curly.

Some of his classmates took their cheek to the next level.

> Tunde, you're too bendy.
> Your sandwiches are weird.
> What's up with that nose anyway?

And, because they were only juniors and hadn't had much life experience at all, they steered clear of Tunde. They left him alone so much, in fact, that he got used to it.

Term dragged on and Tunde started to suspect that he'd be on his own for the rest of his school days. No one to talk to or play games with or even just to share a bag of crisps with. He **loved** crisps. Everyone at junior school did.

In fact, one Halloween, Tunde convinced his mum to make him a costume from bags of salt and vinegar crisps. That night he'd gone out trick-or-treating and by the time he'd reached the corner, his entire costume had been **CHOMPED** by neighbourhood kids who wouldn't normally come near him. That night when he got home, Tunde made a Ways to Make Friends list note for himself:

1. Ask Mum to make me school uniform made of tasty snacks.

It was a short list but a positive sign . . .

But he could never convince Mum to get round to it. Tunde was convinced to his very soul that he was doomed to a dull future of long and lonely school days 'til the end of time, amen.

Then, one day, Justin Walsh (who never spoke to him) approached him in the playground and handed him an envelope. Tunde opened it and inside was a party invitation. This came as a big surprise – to Tunde this was like seeing a giraffe on roller skates. Invitations from his classmates were a rare thing indeed.

Justin scowled, stared at his feet and said in a miserable

manner: 'You've got to come to this. It's my birthday party. There's gonna be games an' cake an' sandwiches an' that.'

Then Justin turned and stomped off, looking like Grumpy McGrumpwort of Grumpsville.

Tunde didn't mind the oddness of the invitation. He was too busy feeling happy. He was going to a party! YAAAAAAY!

Finally, the big day arrived; Justin Walsh's party was happening over at Treetop Adventure Park, which was famous for fun, games, go-karting, lasers and far too many fizzy drinks and crisps. In the car ride, Tunde felt a bit nervous. Would he miss his parents? Would he be lonely? Would anyone talk to him? But as soon as he arrived and got inside, he saw that his fears were unfounded. All his classmates had gone from being gentle little lambs to over-excited wolf kids! All of them were running around, howling and yelling way too much for that time of the morning. Most were red-faced, sweaty and kept having to lie down after each game, to recover from having this much FUN!

Tunde kept overhearing conversations like:

'Did your card say "Games, Cake and Sandwiches"?'

'Yeah, did yours?'

'Yeah, man. I love games.'

'I love cake. I can take or leave sandwiches.'

'I'll have yours if you don't want 'em.'

And then his classmates would run off and lay siege to some other dangerous piece of play equipment. Tunde had the best morning ever! They played ELECTRO TAG, INTERGALACTIC HIDE, SEEK AND DESTROY. They also gave LUCY'S LASER

MISSION and **ARCTIC ZOMBIE QUEST** a try – and that was just in the first half-hour. And at last, he was having fun with the other kids – Justin included. In fact, Tunde made Justin laugh several times, even if Justin did keep putting his hand over his mouth to hide his glee at Tunde being laser-tagged or chomped on by a snow-zombie.

Mr and Mrs Walsh sat in Parents' Central, a reception area where the mums and dads drank cups of tea and waited to sort out the after-effects of too much running, jumping, spinning, lasering and galactic annihilation.

If a child needed to throw up, get a tetanus injection, or be bandaged from head to foot, the grown-ups stepped in and took care of their own. The Treetop Adventure Park staff weren't that interested in dealing with the kids. If there was an injury they'd barely look up from their phones to call an ambulance.

At last it was lunchtime, and all the kids were seated around tables and served their meal, which was, yes, a **TOWER** of sandwiches and cake all to be washed down by a gallon and a half of fizzy pop (guaranteed not to contain any natural flavourings whatsoever). Yum-a-rama!

As soon as Tunde sat down, Mrs Walsh rushed over and piled his plate higher with even more sandwiches. Mr Walsh filled his glass to the brim with fizzy pop. Tunde was happy, even though all this food could have made the Incredible Hulk have second thoughts. 'Hulk not that hungry . . .'

Then they started asking him questions.

'Tunde . . . so . . . that's an African sort of name, isn't it?' asked Mrs Walsh.

Tunde **SLURPED** his drink loudly, thought for a minute and said, 'It's a Nigerian name – Tunde means "Returns" in Yoruba. When they adopted me, Mum and Dad looked at me and thought it was the right name.'

Mr Walsh nodded vigorously. 'So Nigeria, eh? You good at running then? People from Nigeria and those places generally are, aren't they?'

Tunde didn't know why they were quizzing him like this – he was only halfway through his first of an eight-foot tower of sandwiches and they weren't going to eat themselves. However, he was polite and tried to answer their questions politely.

'They're fast,' he said. 'But Jamaicans are probably the fastest!'

He remembered a race he'd watched with his mum and dad, where a Jamaican athlete called Usain Bolt had run the 100 metres so fast, he could have gone round the track again and still beaten the others and had time for a haircut and manicure.

Mrs Walsh wanted to know more about Tunde, though – she kept asking him nosey questions.

'And your mum and dad, Mr and Mrs Wilkinson – how are they? I remember you had all that trouble with your toilets, didn't you?'

Tunde nodded. 'That Trouble With The Toilet' had made his family notorious in their neighbourhood.

Their house was very old, and one very rainy summer's day the toilets had flooded, leaked all over the house and run into the street. Eventually the mess was cleaned up and the smell was just about gone now, but for many years, the Wilkinson home had been known as 'The House That Poo Built'. It was probably another reason why Tunde struggled to make friends at school.

It had been **very embarrassing**. Just like this interrogation by Justin's parents. Tunde looked longingly at his small apartment block of sandwiches, but it felt as though Mr and Mrs Walsh were settling in for even more questions.

Before they could ask anything else, though, Justin came to his rescue. Yes! Justin Walsh, of all people.

'Mum, Dad, leave him alone! He's got to come and play with us lot now. Stop going on at him!'

And that was that – Tunde was free. He grinned at Justin gratefully, picked up a few sandwiches, and ran off with Justin to play in a hall of mirrors, where everyone's faces and noses looked all bent and twisty and scary . . . not just his.

For once, Tunde felt like everyone else.

And he wasn't missing Mum and Dad at all. But then, during the afternoon break, something terrible happened.

They were all once more sat at the large circular wooden tables outside. The sun's rays played in the nooks and crannies of the dining area, peeping between tree shadows and from behind bushes.

Justin strolled up to Tunde. He was sweaty, spotty and his lank, dirty blond hair was stuck to his forehead. He had a litre bottle of orange pop in one hand and a choc ice in the other. Good times. He looked at Tunde and got straight to the point.

'You enjoyin' it?' he asked.

'Yeah, it's brilliant!' Tunde said.

'I know,' said Justin, a bit smugly. 'My birthdays are mega.' He glugged on his pop for a moment, burped and wiped his mouth. 'It's only cos – well, Mum and Dad invited you. Not me,' said Justin cheerfully. 'I mean, we never talk to each other at school, do we? But Mum and Dad said I should invite you – they said they never see you at any of the other parties and . . .'

Justin stopped and frowned because his mother was signalling him from afar. It was time for the piñata. Justin ignored his mother and finished telling Tunde why he was there.

'Yeah, it's cos they felt sorry for you. Anyway, you should—' But before he could finish his sentence by saying, '. . . hurry up and finish, my dad's made a model of the orange ex-president and we're gonna hit it with baseball bats 'til it busts open and tons of sweets fall out!' – Tunde had stood up and walked off. He got his coat and left without saying thank you or goodbye to anyone. He was going home. No one would miss him. They didn't really want him there anyway.

Tunde **TRUDGED** down the driveway, out the gate and then along the main road and beyond. The further away Tunde got from the party, the calmer he felt. He began to enjoy the gentle breeze and the sound of the birds as they flew overhead. But the longer the walk went on, the more he began to realize that he was very lost indeed.

By the time he reached the motorway bridge, Tunde had no idea where he was. He started to cry. Perhaps he had taken offence too quickly at what Justin Walsh had said. Perhaps Tunde should have just shrugged off the insult. Now he was lost, alone and a bit frightened.

He'd been out for long walks before and always found his way home. But now he'd been walking for at least an hour and had not seen anything to remind him of his neighbourhood. Not one recognizable landmark in all that time. No giant oak tree split down the middle, no star in the east, no two-headed sheep, nothing.

He walked on, muttering, 'Stupid, stupid, stupid, now you'll never get home.' Then he cried a bit more, feeling even more sorry for himself.

There were ramblers with ski poles hiking their way through the nearby woodlands. Every so often they took photographs of trees and bees and birds and unusually shaped rabbit poo. 'Darling, look, this one's shaped like a fire engine!'

Tunde steered clear – he was feeling more lost and more anxious by the minute.

Then he heard a noise. It was a sudden thunderclap of birds – an aftershock of starlings, swifts and swallows, all vying for attention as they swooped and circled each other. Tunde looked up muttering, 'S'all right for you, you can probably see my house from where you are.'

He trudged on, crossing another motorway bridge, desperately looking for something that might lead him home.

The sky began to darken with the darkest of dark grey clouds he'd ever seen . . . and then:

MASSIVE raindrops the size of Volkswagens fell and soaked him instantly. Now he was miserable, lost, alone and wet.

Tunde lifted his face to the sky and yelled, 'I just wanna go home!'

And then, it happened.

He looked up at the sky, and saw thousands of starlings, swifts and swallows swooping and whirling and twirling, and then eventually forming into a giant, ornate, almost calligraphic arrow . . . which then proceeded to point in a north-west direction.

The ramblers, hundreds of metres away, lost interest in the fire-engine-shaped rabbit droppings and pointed their lenses at the sky, taking multiple pictures of the pointing, swarming birds, probably thinking, Now that's a shot for the local papers!

Directly beneath the directorial murmuration, Tunde laughed with joy. The birds were showing him the way home! He started to run in the same direction as the arrow pointed, across main roads, through back gardens, jumping over fences, through allotments, down side streets, alleyways, under washing lines, over compost heaps, through bouncy castles, side-stepping early evening barbecues, until, eventually, as if by magic, he found himself a few hundred metres away from the familiar house with the big garden on the outskirts of the village.

Home.

His trouser legs were muddy, messy, even torn in places, and he was sweaty and a little bit whiffy, but he had reached home in one piece.

Tunde looked up at the feathered arrow above his head and yelled, 'THANK YOU!' and it **DISSOLVED** into a thousand individual birds, all winging their way back to their nests.

He sprinted up the road, through the gate and up the garden path. The front door flew open and an anxious Ron stood there waiting.

'Where the heck have you been, Tunde? I've had Justin Walsh's mum on the phone, screaming blue murder.'

Then Ruth was there, usually so calm and logical, now all red-nosed, red-eyed, with a sopping hankie in her right hand. She'd been worried sick. Tunde knew this, because she said:

'I'VE BEEN WORRIED SICK! Where've you been, Tunde? You've been gone for hours. You could've been eaten by bears or cows

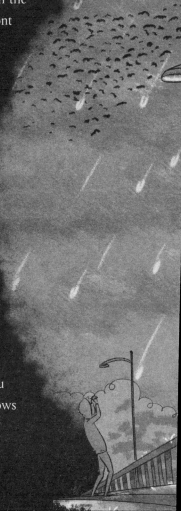

or those grey things with the tails . . . They eat nuts. Ron, what is it I'm thinking of?'

Tunde's dad thought for a moment and replied, 'Meerkats? Otters? Mongeese?'

Tunde muttered, 'Squirrels?'

His mum exploded, 'YES, SQUIRRELS! You could have been devoured

by squirrels, a big gang of them, and once they get the taste of human flesh they don't go back to nuts, you know.'

Ron, now mightily relieved, patted Tunde on the shoulder.

'Come on, let's get you inside. You need a bath, and we need to throw all these clothes in the bin.' He took Tunde's arm and led him away. 'I see deodorant in your future!'

They both laughed as they climbed the stairs. Meanwhile, Ruth looked out the kitchen door scanning the horizon for man-eating squirrels. Not seeing any, she gave a 'Humph' and slammed the door.

That was Tunde's first encounter of the winged kind – but it wouldn't be his last.

3
BIG SCHOOL

The bird-arrow incident happened ages ago and had been mostly forgotten by everyone, including Tunde. By the time he was at big school, he had friends and was coping just fine. There was some bullying to be dealt with on a daily basis, thanks to Quinn and his devoted army, but on the whole, Tunde felt that things at school were going as well as could be expected.

Things at home, though, started to get **weird**.

Tunde's parents had always been reliably, irritatingly, consistently, boringly, **the same**. But when Tunde turned eleven, **they changed**.

Not in big ways. Ruth still cooked her eccentric meals (jerk cashew nuts and seeds? locust trifle?) and Ron still pottered in his oversized genetically modified vegetable garden. They still thought their son was the best boy in the world. They still told him stories about all the great people out there doing great things and all the ways he could make himself and them proud.

And both Ron and Ruth insisted that being kind was the most important thing, and to ignore the bullies.

But Tunde had an inkling, just a gut feeling . . . he knew that something was very wrong.

They were treating him differently, always watching him, and when Tunde caught them staring, they'd look away guiltily. Even weirder, they'd stopped teasing Tunde, and Ron had even stopped making his pathetic Knock-Knock jokes. Tunde missed them so much, he went out to Dad in the garden, scratched his head, hitched up his pants and said:

Dad, Knock, knock.

Who's there?

Dishes.

Dishes who?

Dishes the police, we have the building surrounded!

And the silliest, and Tunde's absolute favourite:

Knock, knock.

Who's there?

Etch.

Etch who?

Bless you!

But after a couple of half-hearted attempts, his dad just stared at him and said he had to do some work before dinner. His mum seemed more tired too. She was still loving, still made him do homework and moisturize his skin and condition his hair, but something seemed off. She looked sad. 'Are you OK, Mum?' asked Tunde one night, when they were stacking the dishwasher.

'Of course, love,' she said. 'Just tired. Lots of work.' That was true – his mum was working very hard. She put in lots of late nights at The Facility and at home in her computer room. But something still felt wrong. And then suddenly there were the weird new rules. His parents had always liked rules, but before they'd always made sense – rules like:

- Treat people how you want to be treated, or
- Lights out by nine, or
- Never eat yellow snow.

But now there were new ones.

Like, Tunde wasn't allowed to run any more. The minute he turned eleven, his mum and dad had simply forbidden it. And Tunde loved to run. When running, his face would light up, like the illuminations at Blackpool. He would have a mile-wide grin on his face, and the faster he ran the more he smiled. It was the one thing he could do better than anyone else. He tried convincing them with a cheeky grin. 'It's your knees,' his mum said. 'They can't handle the strain.'

'And your toes,' said his dad. 'They're all wrong for running. It could cause long-term damage.'

Tunde had stared at his knees and his toes, baffled. They looked perfectly normal to him.

'Why don't I just try a gentle jog to see?' he said.

'No!' yelped his mum and dad together.

'And while you're at it,' said his mum, 'No jumping, skipping, hopping or throwing. And don't pick up anything heavy.'

'But how am I going to explain that to Mr Grierson? He'll

45

notice if I stop doing PE,' said Tunde. He was scared of Mr Grierson, who was built like a block of flats.

'You can do PE,' his mum said. 'Just . . . slowly. Without any running.'

'But Mum . . .'

Then his dad crouched down and looked Tunde in the face with a serious expression.

'Tunde, this is very, very important. Do you understand? You are not to run or do any sports for the foreseeable future. Promise us.'

Tunde promised, even though he didn't understand. And because he loved his parents, he did his best to keep it. But as the months went by, Tunde grew jealous of all his classmates. He kept showing up to watch football, cricket, hockey and swimming practice, but it wasn't the same without being able to join in. It was so frustrating.

But eventually, the choice was taken out of his hands. One day he was forced to run for his life after school – and that was how he met Nev Carter.

Nev was the under-13s football captain, cooler than a penguin on skis licking an ice lolly. He had short dreadlocks, one eyebrow and bandy legs but, even though he was twelve years old, he played football as though he'd been bitten by a RADIOACTIVE Raheem Sterling.

In other words, Nev had mad TALENT on the football pitch; he was probably the best player in the school, despite being so young. Whenever he played, everyone would show up to support the team, and whenever he scored, they would scream until they were bright blue in the face. Nev also called everyone 'bruv', 'mate', 'cuz' and 'fam'. No one knew why – but he made it work.

One night, Tunde was watching a heated footie match against St Ethelred's School for Boys (who wore a strange purple and orange strip with a tie-dye effect that Jiah said was, quite frankly, rubbish).

Nev had scored a hat-trick and had been chaired off the pitch by his fans; Tunde watched in envy, trying to imagine what it would be like to be so popular. It must be like having a number one hit record, or winning an Oscar for the fifth time, or having a basketball shoe named after you. Tunde's **brain boggled** at the possibilities.

And as Tunde stood there with his mind expanding, he was pushed to the ground. **BAM!**

He looked up. Quinn Patterson stood above him, sneering. 'Having a little daydream, Beaky?'

Billy Willis sniggered. 'Yeah – Nev Carter your hero, is he?'

Sanjay spat on the ground, just missing Tunde's hand. Quinn yanked Tunde to his feet, grabbed him by his ear and said, 'Let's play a game, everybody! We know Mr Beakeriffic doesn't like runnin', so let's make him. We'll give you a head start.'

Sanjay, Pauly and Billy cheered, and Tunde squirmed in Quinn's grip.

'Get off me!'

Quinn simply ignored him and carried on. 'I'll count to

fifty, but if we catch you, prepare to be **WEDGIFIED** and, just for the viewing pleasure of the folks at home, a head-first bog dunk.'

With that, Quinn contemptuously let go of Tunde's ear and began counting.

'One, two, seventeen, twenty-eight, thirty-seven . . .' The others laughed, knowing what the punchline was going to be: Tunde Wilkinson was gonna get thwacked. But Tunde was already running out of his skin, and Quinn, now bored with counting, was in **HOT PURSUIT**, followed by his lurching gargoyle-like crew. They weaved in and out of vehicles in the car park, hooting, yelling and screaming like an angry mob. Tunde dodged, ducked and danced in, out and round. No knee pain, no back pain, no hip pain at all. In fact, this felt great. And though he was desperate to get away, he was feeling . . . fantastic.

Meanwhile, Nev Carter watched the whole thing from an upstairs changing-room window. He was impressed as he saw Tunde swerve between a parked Beetle and the bushes, bypassing lamp posts and litter bins, even running along the top of the wall at one point, seriously risking falling and breaking every bone in his body. Nev watched as Tunde raced to the bus stop, just as the 472 was about to depart. Quinn and co. arrived seconds later. They kicked the bus stop and yelled at Tunde as he grinned through the back window of the departing double-decker. Nev could only think to himself, *Wow, that kid with the big hooter can really run, bruv!*

And the very next day at school, he approached Tunde at lunch, asking if he could sit.

Tunde couldn't believe it! Nev Carter sat next to him! He pinched himself and tried to listen – this was EPIC. 'Listen. Tunde yeah? Bruv – you need to be playin' football for the school!'

Tunde couldn't believe it. This was the greatest moment. Of. His. Life! Join the football team? He muttered the word 'WHAAAAAAAAAAT???' under his breath. He wanted to faint, but managed to keep calm . . . just about. No one had ever asked him to do something like that before. He stammered out a reply:

'But I can't play – not like – well, no one can play like you – I mean – you can, obviously – but – I'm just . . .'

'Mate, I'm sure you'll be epic! All you have to do, yeah, is play like you, fam. You do you. You made Quinn and that lot look stupid yesterday. Cuz, you'd be mint on the team, think about it.'

So, Tunde did think about it. But he didn't tell anybody, he probably didn't have to because from that moment on, if you were looking for the school's top goal scorer at lunchtimes, you'd find him with Tunde Wilkinson, debating the merits of orange juice versus Ribena, lime-flavoured KitKat versus normal KitKats, Wonder Woman versus Black Widow . . . or the Smurfs versus them lot in Avatar. (Nev was a big fan – 'I know they're both blue, fam, but the Avatar posse are stoosh, y'get me?')

However, despite this new friendship, Tunde made it

crystal clear that he was forbidden to take part in any sports whatsoever. His mum and dad were being army-level strict about it. But Nev was like a zombie dog with a human leg bone – he just wouldn't let go.

'Nah, nah, nah, bruv, this could be the makin' of you! I'll ask Grierson to put on a suit, go round yours and smile at your parents. That should more than do the trick, innit?'

Tunde begged him not to do that. For one thing, Mr Grierson spat when he talked – that would put Mum right off. And another thing – if anyone was going to convince his mum and dad to let him play football, it would have to be Tunde.

On the bus home, he ran through a number of ways he might persuade his parents into allowing him to try out for the football team:

SCENARIO A:

He could get off the bus early, pick some flowers on the way home, then present them to his mum in the office upstairs and, as she cooed over this surprise bouquet, he'd just casually change the conversation. 'Mum, I'm thinking of joining the school football team. Yes, those flowers do smell lovely, don't they? Gorgeous! Just like you, Mumsy. By the way they're called Agapanthus: Wakanda Forever!'

SCENARIO B:

He might try bonding with his father. Maybe, when he was in his shed, trying to somehow get a large marrow to taste like mackerel for some reason, Tunde could pretend to be interested. 'Hmmm, it's marrow-y and mackerel-y, delicious – you might be on to something here, Pops . . .' and then: 'Dad, what about me playing for the school football team?' But his imagination immediately provided the answer to both scenarios.

In the first one, Mum jams the flowers in the bin, steam comes out of her ears, her eyes suddenly turn blood-red, and she screams, 'No sports in this family EVER. Go to your room and stay there 'til you're thirty-five!'

And in the second one, Dad breathes hellfire, smashes the marrow to smithereens with a nearby lump hammer, and says very quietly, 'What have I told you about football? The answer's NO! You've made me ruin the Mack-Marrow we were gonna have for our tea! Go to your room and stay there 'til you're thirty-five!'

Tunde rubbed his eyes. What was he thinking? By the time he got home, he was exhausted. In the last five minutes of the journey home he'd come up with at least fourteen more imaginary scenes to convince his parents to let him do sport. And every single one ended with him locked in his room 'til he was thirty-five.

He sat at the tea-table, worn out from all this constant thinking, looked at his mum and dad, and just said it: 'Mum, Dad, the best footballer in school thinks I should try out for the team. What d'you think?'

He could hear low birdsong in the trees outside the window as he waited for an answer.

Interestingly, there was no big explosion, no volcanic flames from nostrils, no blood-red eyeballs. Both parents just looked sad and shook their heads. Dad was the first to speak. 'Look, Tunde – we want you to be happy, we want you to do everything all the other children do. But we don't want you to do anything that might endanger you, or anyone else for that matter.'

Tunde rubbed his head. 'What do you mean, endanger? I don't know what you mean.'

Outside, the quiet birdsong from the trees grew sharply in volume.

Ruth spoke now. 'Darling, you're very, very special to us. We've watched you grow and seen you become faster, bigger

and stronger.' She paused for a while, trying to think of how to say this carefully. 'We just think that if you were to be in any sports team, you might put everybody else at a disadvantage. Maybe cause injury . . .'

His dad nodded in agreement – as far as he was concerned, the conversation was over.

But, Tunde didn't understand what they were saying, or why, and for the first time in his entire life, he was **FURIOUS** with them.

The birdsong outside the kitchen window had now become much louder – **SCREECHING** and **CHITTERING** now. Tunde stood up, clearly very angry. Ron and Ruth (very unused to this version of their son) looked at him as if he had just grown another head. This was a first. 'Son?' Ron said. But Tunde was not in the mood. 'It's not fair! I behave myself, do my chores, my homework. I do everything you say, and I don't care that it's BORING. But I do want to do what other kids do, to make the boring bits OK, and you won't let me – it's NOT FAIR!'

He **BANGED** the table again. Hard. Everything jumped six inches in the air.

Just then, five crows flew into the window and **SMACKED** loudly into each other as they hit the glass – **thump thump thump thump THUMP!** An alarming thing to witness. The crows lay on their backs, looking up in a daze at the little cartoon humans flying in circles over their heads.

Tunde's mum and dad were in shock; to be honest, so was Tunde. He had crossed a line, but he couldn't go back – so he stood there and waited for whatever was next.

Ron stood up, looked Tunde in the eye and said, 'Go to your room. And just think about how you've spoken to us.' Now because this was said with no anger, just disappointment, Tunde stopped and was ashamed. He ran out of the room, raced upstairs, pushed his bedroom door open, **SLAMMED** it

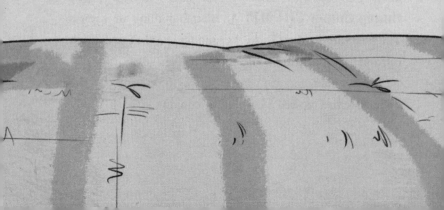

shut and sat on the bed, fighting tears. He didn't know what to do. He tried to play his video game but it didn't help to take his mind off things.

So instead he just lay there for a while, almost in a trance, staring at the astronaut wallpaper and superhero posters that adorned almost every available surface, and he thought for a very long time. And when he'd stopped being cross with himself and his mum and dad, he knew exactly what he was going to do at school the next day . . .

4
SPORTS DAY

Tunde slept and dreamt of deep, dark, starlit space. There was an absence of everything and he was somehow at its centre. He could see himself radiating heat – there was **SMOKE** coming from **HIS** body, and now he was glowing, like a boy-sized sun.

He woke himself up and patted his skin experimentally in case he was on fire, but he wasn't. He gave a sigh of relief, shook his head and didn't give it any more thought. He was excited as he leaped out of bed, and then tiptoed to the bathroom and showered before putting on his clothes and sneaking out of the house like a pre-teen cat burglar.

Tunde was excited because it was Sports Day and he was going to do whatever it took to be involved. Not only that – he just knew he was going to win, he could feel it in his bones. There was a **thrumming determination** careening around his nervous system like an out-of-control driverless coach with a brick on the accelerator. *He was going to win.*

And he was doing all this without the permission of his parents.

Now, like most of us, Tunde knew that the majority of mums and dads were just plain odd. Davy Blenkinsop's dad wore a hat indoors all the time. Annette Lily's gran sang Abba songs in Polish most days in her back garden, and Jordan Tagoe's PARENTS had a house-trained horse . . . and they lived in a first-floor flat.

But — there was nothing *that* weird about Tunde's parents . . . as far as he knew. He knew where they worked and that they did 'sort of science-y stuff' there, but that was it. Here's what Tunde didn't know about where Ron and Ruth worked . . .

The true story of The Facility starts during World War Two —

Wait. Before we get on to that, it's important to understand something.

First and foremost: Belief is important.

For most of us, it's vital to believe in something, whether it's the power of love or kindness, or even the healing effects of a chunky jam sandwich. Because, if we don't believe in something, why is life worth living? We should be grateful for even the smallest of things: cake, music, iPhones, shoes, underpants, hair scrunchies and, of course, funny cat VIDEOS. We should also be grateful for the people who make every effort to do the right thing on our behalf.

People like the founder of The Facility, Professor Emil Krauss.

THIS IS THE BIT WHERE WE TALK ABOUT EMIL KRAUSS: KEEP UP!

Emil Krauss was born in 1911 in Germany. At school, he was a brilliant student and after university became a brilliant and respected young scientist, who had dreams of working on advanced and complex technologies. He became famous in multiple disciplines from physics, chemistry, biology, space travel, human DNA to making the perfect chunky jam sandwich.

He was at the cutting edge of experimentation. However, soon a nasty bunch of people, a political party who'd recently achieved power called the Nazi Party, took an interest in his work. Long story short, these were the bad guys and they (among others) began a war that raged across Europe and eventually the world. When they saw the kinds of things that Krauss could do in a lab with a test tube, some electrodes and some radioactive particles, they immediately decided that he should come and make terrifying weapons of war for them.

But Krauss was (thankfully for us) a decent human being; he decided that he didn't want any part in their war. And so, with the help of friends and a measure of good luck, he made a daring plan to escape from Germany across the English Channel to Dover . . .

His plan worked! In 1941, Krauss made his escape solo. This involved stowing away in a ship's hold, sleeping in a crate of women's clothing, swimming thirty miles to shore in a ball gown, then stealing a child's rusty bicycle for the slowest recorded escape to London, ever. But, still, he made it!

Soon Krauss was able to buy some men's clothes and find secure lodgings; at last he was free. And then, eventually, peace was declared.

He soon found himself at the **Prime Minister's house in Westminster** – the beating heart of British politics, talking to a gathering of world leaders passionately about his wartime experiences and how things needed to change if the world was to have a future at all.

The world leaders all agreed that wars had to end and,

impressed with this sparky, hungry young genius, they asked Krauss what it would take to find a lasting solution.

Krauss stroked his unkempt beard for just a moment, before declaring, 'An end to all war? That, my friends, will take **considerable** time and investment.'

And so, after months of discussion, a unanimous decision was reached – they would do whatever they could to stop wars of any kind ever happening again, and give Krauss access to several billion dollars to figure out a lasting solution using future technologies.

So, they all poured money into the creation of a top-secret complex within which Krauss could work, undisturbed, with colleagues carefully **selected** from all over the world – all of them with one thought in mind: Make the world a better place . . . **by any means necessary**.

There were, of course, several missteps along the way . . . certain . . . **MISTAKES**.

Like the mutated talking monkeys who hijacked a second-hand Suzuki pick-up truck with a cracked engine block and tried to spirit themselves away by ferry to Norway.

Or the highly sensitive artificial intelligence network that hacked into the White House computer system and tried to get itself voted in as President.

Or the super-evolved salmon that almost destroyed the Cotswolds.

These incidents had been dismissed as poppycock, piffle and conspiracy theories by the media. And, for a decade or so, things *had* been a great deal quieter. There were *still* wars happening but they were smaller, nowhere near as big as before.

Until twelve years before this story starts.

Twelve years ago, Krauss was getting cranky. He was now nearly a hundred years old. And, despite the anti-ageing cocktails he'd created at The Facility, which made him look a constant and quite healthy fifty-ish, he wasn't feeling his best.

Why? Well, it all stemmed from the **EXTRA-DIMENSIONAL EXPLORATION UNIT**.

The E.D.E.U. was a very secret division of The Facility and they were on the verge of discovering something extremely important indeed. They had been carefully observing dimensions other than ours for threatening non-Earth-based activity.

You see, since, well, way before *you* were born, they had been interested in space travel to the moon, then Mars and then, eventually, beyond our solar system. More recently, they had been exploring . . . other dimensions.

'Is there life on other planets?' wasn't the question any more.

Now it was: 'Is this dimension the only one out there? Are there other planes of existence? And if so, do they have supermarkets?'

They scanned for signs of life using such complex mathematical procedures that, if you tried to understand, would turn your hair green and make your back teeth explode.

All you need to know is that their efforts **worked**.

Because one day, after days, months and years searching for other dimensions, they only went and flippin' found one!

That night, Krauss wrote in his journal:

We are seeing miracles almost every day! Our scanners are filming dead planets, exploding stars. Pyramid-shaped satellites. Extraordinary!

A month later he wrote:

We're now receiving images of warfare between what look like bizarre cat-creatures and some kind of humanoid bird beings. How is this possible? They are technologically superior to us.

Krauss's **SECOND-IN-COMMAND** at The Facility was called Marcus Humphries. Humphries was a brilliant scientist – but he made Krauss uneasy.

One day he jotted this in his journal:

Marcus is hungry for success, power, money and a Hollywood biopic of some sort. He might as well wear a large hat with a neon sign that says, HELLO, I AM VERY CLEVER, and perhaps trousers with ALSO VERY AMBITIOUS down the sides.

Humphries had all sorts of ideas for how they could make

a ton of money from alien tech, but each time he spoke to Krauss about it, he'd be told no. Marcus was continually and grievously disappointed.

Krauss knew that one day this might become a real problem. But he thought, through conversation and encouragement, he could help Marcus understand how to make the world a **better place** for everyone through science. Not just Marcus Humphries.

They would meet in Krauss's office for daily catch-ups and watch footage of the new dimension and their discoveries. It soon became clear that these creatures were engaged in a never-ending battle – both evenly matched.

One day, they were observing one such fight. Humphries was thrilled and yelled at the screen, 'Look at that! Cat and bird warriors firing **blasters** and laser beams at each other! Who needs to go to the pictures – I could watch this all day!'

Krauss sighed and said, 'Marcus, these creatures are hell-bent on destroying each other. Our **mission** here is about keeping the peace on Earth. If we could instigate some kind of treaty between these most warlike of creatures, then perhaps we **could** learn how to bring the same effect here.'

Humphries pursed his lips, considered the import of Krauss's words, and then responded:

'Yeah, I mean . . . we could do that . . . Or we could snatch one of their ships, steal all their stuff and make billions, baby!'

Krauss pinched the bridge of his nose and sighed again, heavily.

'Marcus,' he said gently. 'These highly developed beings

might take unkindly to humans hijacking their ideas. We've already seen how readily they engage in violence.'

Humphries thought for a minute and then said:

'You're right about the violence – we've seen them vaporize hundreds of each other's ships over and over again. They're not that **evolved** . . . they still like hitting each other with things . . .'

Krauss gave a little smile. 'Not that different from us then.'

Meanwhile, Humphries had a plan. He worked the hardest he'd ever worked in his life. For a month, he slept under his desk and brushed his teeth with a finger and some soap whilst concocting mega-quantum mathematical equations that would make even Einstein break into a sweat. He ate more than his weight in sugary snacks, and got through several hundred calculators.

He and his team were experimenting with teleporting inanimate objects from one place to another by making a physical fold within a black hole. Humphries called it the **BLACK HOLE SNARE**.

One day, Humphries ran all the way to Krauss's office. He didn't even bother to knock, just flung the door open.

'We've done it! The team and I have figured out how to manipulate the 'Cats' into position in order to utilize the Black Hole Snare! Which means – in theory – that we'll be able to jump them from their intended destination to here.' He panted some more. 'What do you think? Shall we do it?'

Krauss frowned thoughtfully.

'What if something goes wrong? They might attack.'

Humphries grinned like a cat who'd found the keys to a dairy.

'We have a Dimensional Reception Portal prepared, complete with extra-strength anaesthetic mist which we'll pump into the room as soon as we've got them. They'll be fast asleep in seconds, by which time we'll have them locked up and whisked away to the observation units – room service and manacles included **free of charge**.'

Krauss looked at him and stroked his grey, unkempt beard. 'This had better work.'

And he went back to the papers on his desk.

That was all the encouragement Humphries needed. He ran back to the **subterranean** level as if superglued to a skyrocket. This was it. His big moment.

And it had to work.

A few days later, they had their chance. Marcus ushered Krauss into the Portal Room's observation deck, through the huge, titanium, **voice-activated door**. Marcus ordered a final check of the equipment and smiled lovingly towards tubes of tranquillizer mist that he'd had built into the surrounding walls.

'Is this it?' asked Krauss quietly.

'This is it,' said Marcus, his eyes shining.

He instinctively reached for Krauss's hand and held it as the countdown began. And, then, abruptly – there was an insistent **PING! PING! PING!** This was it! Extra-dimensional activity detected. Black Hole Snare activated. Fold triggered. There was a blinding flash of yellow lightning and . . .

There, in their midst, was a . . . large space pod.

It was much bigger than they'd imagined from the digital footage they'd seen and quite unlike anything any of them had ever seen before. Colourful sparks and even **BLACK SMOKE** flew from its outer shell as it came to rest. The entire team on the observation deck held their breath, waiting. Silence. No pulse blasts or lasers shot from within.

Next, the hustle and flow of intense activity increased as, on to the lab floor poured **fifTY TECHNICIANS** and Facility operatives. They surrounded the ship's hatch, everyone armed to the teeth.

Noticing the weaponry, Krauss was **furious**. 'What is this, Marcus? Some welcome to our Earth this is! We hijack their ship and then greet them with more guns than the **SPANISH ARMADA**?'

Humphries shook his head. His eyes were still gleaming as he watched the extra-terrestrial vehicle. 'We wouldn't want to be caught out, Emil! We can explain that we mean no harm . . . as soon as we've intercepted and **incarcerated** them.'

Donning their masks and then signalling to each other to proceed, the operatives stepped forward for their first proper encounter with an alien life form.

They approached the spaceship door and waited for it to

open for them and, after the briefest pause, it did.

The ship shimmered for a moment and immediately there was an opening in which a large humanoid, at least eight feet tall, stood, cradling something in its arms. It was a giant egg.

5

ACTUAL SPORTS DAY

Right, now you know all about The Facility, and what happened twelve or so years ago, we can return to the present day: Sports Day at *St Pritchett's school.*

Tunde hadn't told any of his friends he was signing up for the 1,500 metres, he'd just made sure he was prepared. He had his kit in a rucksack; he'd brought Vaseline to make sure his legs were smooth and shiny in his shorts; he'd cut his toenails, blown his nose and combed his hair. He was ready.

He found Mr Grierson and signed up. The teacher was **pleased** – he patted Tunde on the back, which felt like being smacked by an angry elephant.

Kylie saw them chatting and rolled up. She **WAITED** 'til Mr Grierson was talking to Meera Khan's parents about the joys of the shot-put, then homed in on Tunde.

'What you doin'?' she asked.

Tunde shuffled his feet. 'Just chatting to Mr Grierson.'

'Huh. What about?'

'Um.'

'Only it sounded to me like you were signing up for the 1,500 metres.'

Tunde sighed. 'Fine. Yes, I was.'

Kylie frowned. 'Did you fall on your head? I thought your mum and dad said—'

'I know.'

'Tunde, they told you not to do it for your health and well-bein' – whatever that means. You can't just ignore them. They're your parents. Duh?'

Tunde gave her a hangdog look. 'Why does everybody else get to have fun on Sports Day and not me?'

Kylie just shook her head. 'You're gonna get in trouble, Tunde, and it'll be your own fault. Why are you so scared to talk to them? Mum always says: "Fear is a one-way path to darkness, it leads to anger, then hate, and ends up in **BAD TIMES** for everybody."'

Tunde stared at her.

'Your mum doesn't always say that – that's the purple spiky bloke from **Cosmic Warzone** who says that.'

Kylie shrugged. 'Whatever, he's right. Don't be scared to talk to your mum and dad about whatever this is or you'll hate them for standing in your way and then do something stupid, end up in jail and we won't see you for years and then one day you'll be, like, fifty-eight years old, with warts, and you'll come out of jail and see me and go, "Kyles – you were right," and I'll say, "In your FACE, Wilkinson – you shoulda listened to me in the first place!"'

But Kylie was so involved with her pretend scenario that she hadn't noticed Tunde get distracted halfway through and walk off.

There was a new girl **talking** to Mr Grierson. She'd just put her name down for the 4 x 400 metres. And here's the thing – she looked just like him.

Except she had spiky, blonde Afro hair, even darker skin, and a cool way of wearing her uniform.

Tunde **WALKED** over to her almost in a dream state and **managed** to stumble out a **FEW** words.

'H'lo – I'm Tunde Wilkinson – you new?'

That was as much as he managed, because at that moment, Quinn Patterson and his mouth-breathing goons arrived, all noisy, boisterous and brash.

'Hi!' Billy Willis moved towards her at speed, but she sidestepped him so deftly that he wound up neck deep in the herb garden!

Quinn laughed his head off.

'Ahh, man – that was choice. What's your name?'

The girl grinned at him. 'Dembe Diallo – you?'

Quinn **GRINNED** too and replied, 'I'm Quinn. The doofus up to his bum in parsley, sage, rosemary and poison ivy is Billy, big bloke's Pauly Gore, the dude who's sort of staring at yer in a weird way is Sanjay. Say hello, Sanj, yer makin' me look bad.'

Sanjay continued staring at Dembe in a stunned way. But she ignored him – she was a cool customer, Tunde **thought**.

'You runnin'?' Dembe asked.

Quinn puffed up his chest like a ridiculous red-headed rooster.

'Course I am. 1,500 metres. You?'

Dembe **laughed**.

'The relay, boy! I'm doin' the last leg – "Baton please, *vroom*, see ya!"'

Quinn laughed again and then they all **wandered** off. As if being friendly to new pupils was totally normal for this lot.

Tunde couldn't believe it. This girl who looked exactly like him had just shown up, disarmed Quinn and was now all tight with the gang, like peanut butter and jam on toast. She hadn't even looked at him when he'd said hello . . .

'Did you see that?' Tunde said as Kylie re-joined him. 'That new girl just made friends with Quinn Patterson. I didn't know people did that.'

'Yeah,' said Kylie. 'That's the strangest thing I've seen in a long time.'

Mid-afternoon, post lunch, and Sports Day was under way.

It had been an eventful afternoon.

At the starting line of the 100 metres, Audley Barton, a dead cert to win, collapsed holding his stomach as soon as the whistle blew. Probably because he'd eaten jerk chicken, spicy rice, two portions of mac and cheese, some thick slices of bread, cheese and biscuits and a *choc ice* for lunch. As everyone rushed past him to the finish line, Audley lay there regretting that second portion of mac and cheese. He got up and staggered with tear-filled eyes and a mucus-covered face towards his mum, who ran in the opposite direction, her head bowed in shame as she left the school grounds.

Billy Willis was disqualified from the javelin throw because he **SLIPPED** (or so he said afterwards) and managed to hurl the javelin into the crowd. He told the head teacher that he hadn't meant to throw it at Kit-Kat Price, because if he had, he would have taken better aim. Willis was given a week's exclusion for his cheek.

Kylie had simply smashed the archery competition, leaving everyone in her wake. Boom!

Finally, it was time for the 1,500 metres. Rather nervously, Tunde came out on to the track, dressed in running gear with his number Sellotaped to his chest.

His mates gathered round, but before they could give him a pep talk, Quinn Patterson strolled over.

'Well, well, well. Look who it ain't? Beaky McLeaky, the worst athlete on Earth. I can't wait to leave you in my dust. **This is gonna be great**.'

Quinn strolled away.

'Ignore him,' said Kylie.

'Yeah, you just do you, bruv,' said Nev.

'By my calculations, your odds of beating him are not that good,' said Jiah helpfully. 'But give it your best shot – we're all here for you.'

Tunde sighed. 'Thanks a lot, you guys!' But even though he should have been dreading the race, he felt strangely confident. Like he was finally doing what he was meant to do.

The race was about to start and so he took his position on the starting line. He looked at Quinn Patterson, who sneered; Tunde ignored him.

The starter whistle blew: **TWEEEEEET!**

The next few minutes for Tunde were like a dream.

Tunde lurched forward, and from then on, it felt as though he wasn't running against anybody except himself. The other runners blurred as he left them behind, and he realized he was the happiest he'd ever been. He was smiling, his eyes **SHONE** and – if you looked closely at him – you'd have seen that his feet were hardly **touching** the ground.

Kylie, Jiah and Nev were obviously going wild, but the rest of the crowd cheered themselves hoarse too. It was probably the greatest race they'd seen in school history. Tunde had not only beaten everyone else, he'd lapped the stragglers. Twice.

Quinn Patterson, who had **struggled** and almost kept up with Tunde but lost him two laps in, was red, pink and purple in the face. Like a melting rainbow ice cream.

As soon as Tunde crossed the finish line, Nev, Kylie and Jiah crowded round him.

'You were on fire out there!' yelled Jiah. 'It was like watching the cartoon with that bird that runs on the road – I don't know what it's called, but it was exactly like that!'

Kylie was so **happy** she was almost in tears.

'That was amazing. A-ma-zing! It was like you were running on air, Tunde! You were flying out there – brilliant. You made Quinn Patterson look like a snail trying to move through treacle! I'm so proud of you . . .' She hugged him way too tight.

Nev just stood there with a silly grin on his face, saying 'Cuz . . . fam . . . bruv' repeatedly. It was great. Tunde was shepherded to the long trestle table where he was given his certificate and gold medal by Mr Baxter, the music teacher, and Miss Mooney, who was in charge of all things geography. There were loads of pats on the back from everyone that could reach him and all around him he could hear praise:

'That was ace!'

'Where'd you learn to run like that, Tund?'

'I've never seen anything like that!'

But then he heard, 'If you pea-brains think that was **GOOD**, just wait 'til you see the relay, man.'

Tunde looked over to see Dembe stretching nearby as he

soaked up all that encouragement. This should have been a top moment for him but she was spoiling it.

Before Tunde realized it, he said, 'You haven't even run yet – maybe you shouldn't brag before you've been out there.'

Dembe smirked. 'What? You scared I might hijack all your new little fans? Break your record? Steal your thunder?'

Then, leaving Tunde **spluttering indignantly**, Dembe walked off with Pauly Gore and Billy Willis.

'Well, well, well,' came a nasty voice. 'If it's not the boy wonder.' Tunde turned and swallowed. It was Quinn Patterson, come for payback time. Just then, though, six older boys with red hair and homemade tattoos emerged from behind a tree and began making fun of Quinn.

Their hair and colouring marked them out as his big brothers . . . uh-oh. (Their dad relieving himself behind a nearby rose bush might have been another clue.) They all spoke in quick-fire succession – they used words as weapons and were well-practised . . .

'Ah, Mr Losey McLoser of Loserville.'

'You was awful out there, Quinnbo – did you miss your bus?'

'You were runnin' like you'd messed yer pants.'

'Well something stank out there – an' it wuz you, bro!'

'The beaky Black kid wiped the floor with yer – yer should be ashamed of yerself.'

Tunde watched as all of Quinn's **TOUGH-GUY** bravado melted away.

'Leave me alone, you lot!' he muttered.

But they didn't leave him alone – tough big brothers rarely do. Not one of them let up on making Quinn feel **bad** until he finally snapped. 'I said leave me alone – at least I had a go!'

One of his brothers jumped all over that.

'You "had a go"? You got lapped . . . twice!'

They all repeated a nice, loud **TWICE!**

Then they each took it in turns to punch their younger brother in the arm. Although this was just everyday rough-housing to the Patterson brothers, to Tunde it looked painful. The older ones were laughing but Quinn was red-faced and moist-eyed. All his life, Tunde's parents had taught him right from wrong, and told him stories about normal people who stood up for those weaker than themselves. Somewhere along the line, these stories must have rubbed off on him because, before he could think too hard about it, Tunde sprinted across to the Pattersons and said, 'Pack it in, you lot. You'll hurt him.'

Dennis, the eldest, looked at Tunde as if he was something nasty on the bottom of his shoe.

'Sorry, aardvark-face, did you say something?'

Tunde hesitated. Satisfied, Dennis turned back and kneed Quinn up the bum.

'I said that's enough!' exploded Tunde. 'Leave him alone!'

Confused at Tunde's interference, Quinn glared daggers and said, '**BACK OFF**, Wilkinson! I-I can fight my own battles – don't need your help.'

As if to disprove this last claim, his elder brothers swiftly dragged Quinn away and took it in turns to wedgify him. Tunde watched helplessly.

Kylie, Jiah and Nev joined him.

'That's not right,' said Tunde **miserably**.

'Watching the school bully be bullied? It's awesome,' said

Kylie. 'Best thing to happen all year. I would've filmed it but my phone's run out of battery.'

Tunde shook his head. 'His brothers are worse than he is. If we stand by and let him get bullied, we're no better than he is.'

Nev shrugged. 'Fam, it's none of my business. And none of yours either.'

Tunde just watched as the brothers yanked Quinn by the scruff of his neck off the school grounds and towards the bus stop.

He sighed. 'I just felt sorry for him, I guess.'

'Not as sorry as I feel for you right now,' muttered Jiah. She nodded behind Tunde, who spun around.

His mum and dad were walking towards him. Even at this distance he could tell they were not pleased. His mother's Afro hair blew from side to side with every furious stride. His dad's stern face moved ever closer.

Kylie hissed under her breath:

'Don't forget, Tunde: don't be scared. FEAR is a one-way path to darkness.'

Tunde gulped. Not being scared was easier said than done, especially when it came to his mum.

6

THE SEEKER

The Seeker, as he had taken to calling himself, stared at his reflection in the mirror. He had no idea how many days, weeks or months had passed. Earth time meant nothing to his kind – he knew that it went dark and then light and that had something to do with this planet's moon and sun, but in terms of hours, minutes or seconds, the Seeker was in a bit of a muddle.

His belly told him when **HE HAD TO EAT**, and his instincts told him that the best time to hunt was when darkness fell – he liked to stalk prey in the wooded areas where the smaller creatures lived. The tiny grey ones with the bushy tails were very similar to creatures on his home planet, although this breed did not wear jet-packs and carry blasters, which made them easier to catch.

He had sampled a number of animals in the surrounding habitat and learned a great deal.

He had stalked a large mammal with low-hanging udders, but to no avail. Even when he had managed to take a bite, it simply kicked him several metres away into some bushes and said **MOOOO!** for the longest time, which didn't make sense at all.

The white fluffy furry things that kept saying **BAAA!** were equally unintelligible, looked plump and delicious, but one attempt to taste it taught him it would be best to shave it thoroughly first.

Still, he had managed to survive, here on Earth. But he felt that time was **running out**. He had to find the hatchling. Everyone was counting on him.

He regretted not staying by the Supreme Leader's side at the point of attack; the truth was that he was a coward. He was simply not built for conflict.

No, this particular Seeker was a Furleenian diplomat, tasked with ending the **aeons-long battle** between the Aviaan and the Furleen. The females of both species had wisely come together to push for peace. A worthy task — but one that seemed downright impossible.

Still, recently, he thought that there had been a breakthrough of sorts. Both sides were tiring of war. Those calling for peace were persuasive. He thought that the talks had been going well, and bridges were finally being built. It looked like the Never-ending War might finally, one day soon, come to an end.

There were others who wanted nothing more than for the **conflict to continue endlessly**. It reminded him of the ancient Furleenian saying: 'Some creatures would rather claw and scratch than curl up and purr . . .'

Still, he thought, if he could find the Supreme Leader and his hatchling, then there was hope.

The Seeker studied himself in the mirror once more, lifted his gauntlets and pushed back his hood. He stood **admiring** his reflection; even though he said so himself, he looked fabulous! He had a velveteen face, extraordinarily long and curly whiskers, a perfectly triangular nose, and, when he flashed his teeth, they were elegant, **ivory-white** and razor-sharp. He purred and allowed the sound to roll around his chest and mouth.

There was a noise, and he quickly pulled his hood back up so that his features were once again in shadow; he put the gauntlets back on and waited.

A human male entered and relieved himself at the urinals. The Furleenian nodded and grunted as he had observed others do in such a situation. He kept his face hidden. The man grunted in response.

The Seeker left him to it and strolled out of the toilets, keeping his head down as he passed the receptionist, who muttered gruffly that only members were allowed to use the facilities – 'This IS a private golf club, after all.'

He had no idea what she was talking about and ignored her, darting towards the wooded area. He scrambled up a tree in four or five deft moves, and sat on a thick branch. He purred.

Then he fished around in his cloak and withdrew a box-like device, on which he had been keeping a diary of his time on Earth. He waved a paw over the controls and it lit up; he spoke in his own language.

'I, Juba, designated peacemaker in charge of all peace treaty discussions between the Furleen and the Aviaan, am still hiding in this wooded place of small, tiny beings with long tails, and larger creatures that speak no language except for MOO or Baa which I have difficulty translating. I notice they are not the dominant life form here.

'The superior creatures here are large, mostly pale, ghostly beings. They stalk these wooded areas, repeatedly hitting small circular objects with a stick weapon with some force until this spherical object is propelled to another wooded area featuring a tiny hole. Most of them are not very good at this activity. Perhaps this ritual is how their leaders are chosen.'

He pondered this for a moment, and then continued.

'If I'm to locate the hatchling and the Supreme Leader, I must research my whereabouts, as I am certain my transportation device took me many leagues from their original location. My initial aim is to—'

Before he could finish talking, he heard someone yell 'FORE!' and a small white ball rocketed through the surrounding greenery and hit him in the forehead. **SMACK!**

He almost fell off the branch, yelling, **'OW! OW! NOT THIS AGAIN!'**

Several crows on a nearby branch cawed loudly at this. Almost as if they were laughing.

Juba glared at them, and then scrabbled to regain his composure, reached into his cloak and produced a handful of the white spheres, hurling one into the near distance. He heard the stick-weapon warriors trudging towards the area with the hole in it. He glared at the laughing crows – then had an idea and waved his paw over the recording device once more.

'Juba, you fool! The answer is obvious. Aviaans are connected to all winged things. I must travel further afield, noting any out-of-the-ordinary winged-creature disturbances wherever I go. This is bound to lead me to the Supreme Leader and his hatchling, who must be nearing maturity at some point soon.'

Night fell, and he left that wooded place, under cover of the inky darkness.

He hid on one of their transports. A multi-wheeled thing with two floors and seats under which a supple being such as he could hide.

He got out at the brightly coloured and lit dwelling centre and found his way to a place where, through the windows, he could see many information screens and keyboards (similar to his small translation device) and posters written in the native language. The building had a huge sign carved into it.

He waved the device across it and looked at the screen. The word 'library' appeared with a definition: Custodians of writings for pleasure and information.

The device made a loud noise.

PING!

Almost as if it were taking a bow.

It sounded like a 'library' would have the answers the Seeker was looking for. He slept on a nearby rooftop.

The next day, he headed to the library, walked in and tried not to draw attention to himself. He found a computer, stuck his translation device to the side and started to scan for anything unusual – and PING! Once more his translation device had come up trumps.

If anyone were to glance over his shoulder at his device right now, they would see bars of light scanning newspaper articles and photographs and transforming that information into unearthly squiggles that was actually the Furleenian language.

The Seeker read the article with interest. On screen there was a large photograph of **tiny** birds in an unusual flight formation. The article read:

ARROW IN THE SKY!

Local amateur photographers captured an extraordinary image of a large group of starlings forming themselves into an arrow shape. A representative from the Royal Institute of Ornithology claimed the shot was a fake or an April Fool's joke.

'In actual fact, this particular area has been known to manifest odd instances of bird-related activity . . . However, birds do not, as a rule, form themselves into convenient comedy shapes for the purpose of amateur photographers,' they told this paper. 'Clearly this has been photoshopped by some idiot with too much time on his hands.'

As Juba read on, he felt a rising excitement. This had to be the location! The hatchling had clearly been **DELIVERED** safely and now lived amongst humans. He had communed with the local winged creatures and now, of course, they did his bidding.

And now all he had to do was locate him, activate his enhanced **abilities**, inform him that his father was being held prisoner and that it was their duty to rescue him. Also, and this was of the utmost **IMPORTANCE** to Juba's thinking, the hatchling alone could negotiate the end of an aeons-long war.

Easy.

Juba pressed a button on his gauntlet and a microphone device flipped up from his chin. He spoke:

'Hatchling found. I will send location details and then we should rendezvous, yes?'

He pressed the button again and his mic flipped down. There was work to be done.

GROUNDED, GAMES, GOALS AND GONE

If Tunde had hoped that his parents would be OK with him sneaking into the 1,500-metres race, he was wrong. After attempting to explain just why he'd taken part against their wishes, Tunde was grounded.

Or as Nev said on the phone: 'Bruv, you got **proper told off**, innit?'

The weird thing was, Ron and Ruth had grounded him, but they didn't seem to mind him having his mates over. 'Go ahead and ask your friends,' Ruth had said. 'You should have some company.'

Tunde was confused by this but Nev had just SHRUGGED.

'Bruv, your dad said you was grounded, but we aren't. It din't mean we couldn't come round an' hang out an' that.'

Shortly after that night, Tunde's mum had brought a computer game home. She chucked it on his bed. The game had no box or leaflet or logo or anything.

'Thought you and your mates might like this,' she had said.

It's called S.H.I.P.P.E. Space Fighter. It's a prototype we've been working on. A new game about space fighters. You can play it on your own or with your mates like a team. It's, um . . . not out yet.'

Tunde had stared after her as she'd left. He would have liked to have asked her to play the game with him but she was still angry with him for disobeying her. For the last week, whenever she saw him around the house she'd speak in a Jamaican accent, like her mum used to, and say things like:

'I don't know what kinda house you tink this is, but it is definitely NOT the kinda place where pickney lif' up dem voice to big people an' kick over chair an' ting like him is some kinda man or someting.'

She always sounded scary when she talked like that, so Tunde kept out of her way and let her cool down for a while. Eventually, she stopped giving him *the look*, and now she had given him the game he felt like he was getting his mum back.

So, Tunde showed the S.H.I.P.P.E. Space Fighter game to his friends. He turned it on and a **VOICE SAID**, 'Sentient Hyper-Intelligent Pan-Planetary Entity ready for boarding. Would you like to play?'

At first they thought it was 'basically . . . sub-par'.

'Bruv, what is this, man?' said Nev. 'It ain't even got a logo and it kinda looks homemade.'

'Yeah,' said Kylie suspiciously. 'Is your mum trying to offload some educational rubbish on to us?'

'Listen,' said Jiah. 'Tunde is grounded and so we have to stay here. There's nothing else to do. So we might as well play, yeah?'

They all headed up to his room, Kylie using the super-slow wheelchair-lift that Ron and Ruth had installed just for her.

'Can't your mum tweak this to make it go **FASTER**? This is basically *sub*-sub-par.'

The gang absorbed the basic gaming system quickly. It was almost as if it were designed especially for them. You just put the goggles on, attached the wrist bands and watched the heads-up display, which appeared right in front of you in 3-D and showed you what to do.

Jiah's big maths brain figured out ways **round** different situations for them that made a lot of sense. Kylie was a natural pilot and Tunde and Nev operated weapons systems as if they were born to do it.

The game was enjoyable and made for some hilarious chat.

'On your left, Tunde, on your left – YOUR LEFT!'

'On my left or their left?'

'YOUR LEFT!'

'All right, got it.'

'Response pods at ten o'clock.'

'What? Ten o'clock like on a clock?'

'No, like on your foot!'

'OK, I've got them. T'port now!'

'Gone! Oh yeah – we be **cool**, baby!'

'Who talks like that? Also, I need the toilet. It helps me think.'

'It helps you stink, you mean.'

After a while, the kids couldn't get enough of S.H.I.P.P.E.

Space Fighter. They didn't even have to speak in order to take off, survey their particular area of space and then locate the enemy. They were a team. They **talked** about it all day at school, planned strategies. This game was in their heads, all the time.

Meanwhile, Tunde had done a bad thing. It wasn't stealing a plane or committing a solo bank heist or impersonating a surgeon (though that had crossed his mind from time to time). What he'd actually done was start attending training sessions with the **football** team. Nev had persuaded him to go against his parents' wishes and he had. He didn't want to cause them any more heartache, but he knew what he wanted, and no, it wasn't a multi-level-heart-stoppa-whoppa-burger from the local fast-food joint down the road; he just wanted to play football.

Mr Grierson took him on after one trial. It wasn't like he **had much to lose**; St Pritchett's football team couldn't get any worse. Even with Nev playing at his best, the team struggled near the drop zone at the bottom of the school league.

So Tunde joined the team and he loved every second of it.

There was just one problem – there were some **other** new members on the team too.

One was Quinn Patterson! The other was Dembe. She could kick with either foot and wasn't scared to tackle and get mean during play. Tunde tried to tell her how great she was, but she would ignore him.

'Hey, Dembe! Great tackle!' he would say, and she would

93

look right through him, as though he were a pane of glass.

It was like one of dad's jokes:

Patient: *Doctor, I keep thinking I'm invisible.*

Doctor: *Who said that?*

But it didn't matter to Tunde. He didn't care whether she liked him or not. He was determined to be her friend.

'She's so cool,' he told his mates after practice, watching as Dembe bantered with Quinn.

'Yeah,' said Nev. 'She's a bit pleased with herself but she is good. She always has so much time on the ball.'

'She does pass well,' admitted Kylie. 'Never misses.'

'She's like Ronaldinho,' said Jiah. 'If he had blond spiky hair and was super-sarcastic.'

The only thing that Tunde didn't like about training was Quinn Patterson. He was a complete and utter monster-truck-sized pain in the bum. But Mr Grierson kept picking him for the team because Quinn was **'hungry'** and 'tireless' and 'fearless' no matter how big, scary and wolverine-like their opponents were. He played so rough that during training he even battered his own team.

'We're all on the same side, Quinn,' Mr Grierson kept saying. 'It'd be great if you didn't keep trying to kick your **teammates'** heads off!'

But even during these training sessions, Quinn would argue, cheat, push and yell at whoever was in front of him. To him, everyone was the enemy. And, as far as he was concerned,

Tunde shouldn't even have been on the team. He moaned about it to his mates.

'I can't believe they picked Beak-o-saurus rex,' he muttered. 'I wonder why.'

'Maybe they took pity on him,' said Billy Willis.

'You want me to trip him up and kick him in the shins?' said Pauly Gore.

'Flush his kit down the loos?' said Sanjay Khan.

'Nah, leave it with me. I'll sort it out,' sighed Quinn. 'There must be some reason they picked him. Let's just wait and see what it is.'

As **training** continued throughout the following months, though, it became more and more apparent that the team were improving. With Tunde and Nev up front and Dembe and Patterson as 'chili sauce' ('picking up the ball and **COOKING** up a storm, fam,' as Nev would put it), the team were playing better than they had done in years. Mr Grierson couldn't believe his luck. If everyone got on – and didn't get in each other's way – they could do *anything*.

It also seemed that the more Tunde and Nev played **S.H.I.P.P.E. Space Fighter**, the better they got at football. They developed an instinct whilst kicking the ball back and forth almost as if they could read each other's minds. Instead of passing directly to Nev, Tunde would pass to where Nev would be in two seconds' time.

At last, Mr Grierson decided it was time to try his team out on a real opponent. St Grayson's Jesuit Boys School were coming for a pre-championship match.

If they could just manage to beat St Grayson's, this would bounce them up from the 'Don't mind us, we're **rubbish**' relegation zone.

Then, disaster struck, like a Tasmanian devil in a supermarket fight with a saltwater crocodile.

One day, Nev was displaying his keepy-up skills in the street on the way to the bus stop when, due to a large **AWKWARDLY** placed pebble, he slipped and hurt his ankle. 'Still kept the ball in the air though, bruv, y'feel me?'

The news spread around the school like wildfire. At training that afternoon, Mr Grierson walked on to the pitch in his red school tracksuit, and Quinn Patterson **muttered** loud enough to be heard by everyone in earshot:

'He looks like a blond tomato in trainers.'

Mr Grierson ignored him.

'All right you lot, settle. Nev Carter's sprained his ankle and can't play this week, which means some changes for the match.'

Tunde's heart almost beat out of his chest. He knew he was good when he played with Nev – but what about when Nev wasn't there? Would he fall apart?

'So,' Mr Grierson went on, 'that means, Dembe, you'll play up front with Wilkinson, and Patterson, you can play fast and loose in the middle.'

Dembe **smirked** at Tunde.

'You'll have to work harder with me than you do with Nev,' she said. 'You gotta pass to my feet – not ten metres ahead. I ain't Speedy Gonzalez.'

She saw Quinn scowling at her for talking to Tunde and turned her back . . .

Training stepped up a gear that week. Instead of playing worse without Nev, Tunde came into his own. He played like he'd never played before. He could outrun anyone and out-think them too. He seemed to know what his opponents were **thinking** before they did. He and Dembe worked well together.

Which had the worst possible effect on Quinn, who went from grumpy to absolutely furious, mowing down anyone who was in his path, **teammate** or not.

Mr Grierson noticed, but there wasn't much you could do about Quinn – much like his brothers before him, you just had to grit your teeth and wait for him to leave school. When that happened there'd be a glorious parade with a marching band and **fireworks** . . . and placards reading 'GOOD RIDDANCE, PATTERSON!' and 'NO MORE WEDGIES – HOORAH!'

Mr Grierson wasn't the only one who'd noticed Quinn's behaviour. After practice one day, Dembe found him outside the locker room and tried to talk sense into him.

'Dude,' she said. 'We're on the same team. Just chillax, man. You gave that little kid a black eye.'

Quinn shrugged. 'Surprise, surprise, you're crawling up Beaky's nose too. I guess you look just like him so it's no wonder. *You* chillax. We're not on the same team. I'm playin' for me an' no one else.'

And he got up and tried to storm out.

But as he **reached** the locker-room door, he found Tunde standing in the way. To Quinn's disbelief (and to Tunde's as well) he put a hand on Quinn's **shoulder**.

'Quinn, can't we just forget this and play like a team, yeah? The important thing isn't us – it's winning this match!'

Quinn **shook** him off.

'What do you think you're doing, Beak-brain? Get out of my way. You for real?' Quinn said, and shoved past Tunde. Hard. Dembe and Tunde looked at each other and Tunde shrugged.

'I tried,' he said. 'I guess he's just not interested.'

Dembe sighed, then ran after Quinn. 'Oi, Patterson!' Tunde heard her **yelling**. 'You can be a real jerk sometimes, y'know. No – scratch that – all the time . . .'

'Whose side are you actually on, Dembe?'

'I'm on our side, y'big galoot! The Head's given the whole school the afternoon off to watch this – why don't we just try and win the game for all of us for a change?'

There was a long silence in which Tunde could **IMAGINE** Quinn and Dembe glaring at each other. Then Quinn grunted and raged off **muttering** about traitors and betrayal. Tunde glanced into the corridor and watched Dembe following at her own pace.

Tomorrow's game was gonna be fun.

It was the afternoon of the match and quite a few pupils and teachers gathered around the main pitch. A few parents and interested onlookers formed the rest of the crowd who were abuzz with **anticipation**.

There was someone else in the crowd too. Someone wearing a large coat and hooded cloak, someone with claws shrouded in gauntlets.

The Seeker took his place just as the game began. He wasn't too clear on the rules but he watched keenly as Tunde ran, jumped,

and outpaced everybody on the pitch. It had to be said, the hatchling was playing as though his future depended on it.

And perhaps, though he didn't know it yet, it did.

The crowd went wild. Who knew that Wilkinson was such a star player? Cheers echoed around the pitch.

'Come on, Tunde!'

'Look at Beaky go!'

'Yes, bruv! Yes, yes, yes!' (That was Nev, who was waving from the sidelines.)

Quinn Patterson got increasingly angrier as the game developed. His plan seemed to be to cheat and shoulder people off the ball whenever possible. The referee didn't notice – she was obviously short-sighted – even facing the wrong way when, at one ridiculous point, Quinn tackled Tunde, his own teammate. Mr Grierson slapped his forehead so hard his brains nearly came out the other side.

'What are you doing, Patterson???' he yelled. He was beginning to think it wasn't worth having a wild animal on the team if it kept biting chunks out of his own teammates.

A couple of minutes later, all was forgotten: Tunde scored a totally sick over-the-head, bicycle-kick-style goal and EVERYBODY from St Pritchett's jumped in the air, whooped, hollered and did a variety of dances.

'Yes!' screamed Mr Grierson. 'Yessssssss!'

But the home team's joy didn't last long. St Grayson's main striker, a giraffe-tall, curly-headed boy called Dunster, managed to score two sneaky goals in quick succession. He celebrated by doing flick-flacks, landing on his hands and then kicking back like a donkey. Everyone just stopped and stared in awe.

The whistle blew and everyone breathed a sigh of relief.

'Half-time,' said Mr Grierson. **'Thank goodness.'**

He followed behind the team into the locker room. Everyone ate oranges or digestive biscuits and glugged orange squash. They all had their glum game faces on.

Nev **hobbled** in. Mr Grierson stood in the centre of the room, looking moody as everyone ate.

'Great play, Tunde,' he said. 'Dembe, you too, nice work. But as for the rest of you! What're you doing out there? Get it together! Focus! Play as a unit! Watch each other's backs. The **whole school's** watching us this afternoon. This is our chance to scrape ourselves out of the relegation zone and hold our heads up high for the first time in ages!'

The team hung their heads.

Grierson rounded on Quinn.

'Patterson – you've gotta get it out of your head that it's just you out there. Do yourself a favour. Get the ball to Tunde or Dembe – end of.'

There was a **pause**. Quinn scowled, then Nev couldn't help himself.

'Yeah, Quinn, let Tunde and Dembe put in work and stop being a nincompoop, innit?'

Quinn glared at Nev.

'If you hadn't tripped on a tiny pebble, we'd be in the lead by now, snake-head.'

Nev shook his head, tossing his dreadlocks.

'Well, you ain't got me, y'get me? You lot are on your own. Coach is right – get your head in the game – or we goin' down.'

Quinn opened his mouth to say something mean, but just then the knock came for the end of half-time. The team filed out. Audley Barton patted Tunde on the back, as did a few others. Dembe got up, **glugged** squash from her huge bottle and popped the cap back on.

'You know it's down to us, right? Because, no offence to the rest of them, but they're hopeless.'

Tunde looked at her and nodded.

Dembe gave him one of her rare grins. 'Come on, then. Let's show 'em what we got.'

If St Pritchett's had just been given a mild pep talk, then St Grayson's had clearly been given the kind of team roasting you see in sports movies, where the coach picks up a bin and **throws** it across the room. They were **ENERGIZED**. They were **PUMPED**. They were, it seemed, unstoppable.

For the first few minutes of the second half, St Grayson's ran, jumped, kicked and passed as if they had all been threatened with a transfer to Siberia.

St Pritchett's had to up their game to match the intensity of play and they did reasonably well. The crowd were enjoying themselves, lost in the game.

All except for one.

Juba knew nothing about football and had been getting slightly cold and bored by the end of the first half; but thanks to some reading up he'd done during half-time, he now recognized the patterns of battle and also the warriors. He scanned the pitch for signs of the hatchling.

He found him quickly. The hatchling – who Juba had learned was now known as Tunde from the chanting crowd – was receiving the spherical object from a very agile girl-child, Juba saw. Then a ridiculously tall boy-child with red fur went charging across to rob Tunde of the spherical object. That same boy-child then attempted to kick the spherical object through the posts, but was laughably far from on target.

But the next time the red-furred boy-child attempted to tackle Tunde, the spherical object was flicked up into the air and then Tunde performed once more, a perfect overhead kick and – **BAM!** He'd scored. Through the posts with devastating force.

The crowd went, as he'd read via his translator, *BANANAS!*

Juba nodded slowly. This was definitely the offspring of the Supreme Leader. He was sure of it.

Finally, just minutes before full-time, the scoreboard read 4–4. There was everything to play for, but then the ball landed at the feet of Quinn Patterson, who was as red-faced and miserable as someone who'd just **flushed** a winning lottery ticket down the bog by mistake.

Quinn ran, jinking from left to right, looking in vain for the shot, which he did not have.

Mr Grierson spied Tunde free near the halfway line and yelled:

'Tunde!'

Everything slowed right down as if they were all running hip deep through thick mud.

Quinn looked up, saw Tunde just standing there and heard the whole school yelling and screaming at him to pass.

The referee looked at her watch.

Quinn hesitated, grinned ruefully, and then . . . kicked the ball straight up in the air.

Mr Grierson howled with rage. The ref **looked** at her watch once more and began to raise her whistle. But, at that moment, Tunde leaped into the air, meeting the ball at the peak of its trajectory, flicking his head just so, and smashed it into the back of the net. Everything sped up now:

It was a goal. The whistle blew.

Everyone was in shock.

Everyone was staring.

Everyone seemed to ask the same question simultaneously. *How had Tunde Wilkinson got that high to head the ball in the back of the net like that?* And they were also asking: *Why hadn't he come back down yet . . . ?*

Tunde didn't notice for a moment. He was too **happy**. He had scored the winning goal! He had been man of the match! He had proven, once and for all, that he was meant to be there. St Pritchett's weren't going down to the rubbish league any more . . . And the sunlight shone brightly on his wings and all was well in the . . .

Hang on.

His *wings*??

Tunde looked to his left and his right and he saw that

104

massive wings had suddenly burst out from the middle of his back and upper shoulders.

Down below, he saw Jiah, Kylie and Nev watching the whole thing. Their mouths were **OPEN WIDE** and he knew exactly what they were thinking, because it was the same thought in his own mind.

OMG. Tunde's got wings, man!

And they weren't just any old wings either. They were beautiful, majestic and powerful wings – he barely needed to flap to stay in the air. He just continued to float, like a human-shaped bird of prey, using the air-currents to linger as if by some kind of arcane magic, kept aloft by an **UNSEEN** breeze.

The entire crowd watched, gibbered, jabbered, prattled and rattled. Quinn Patterson and Mr Grierson included. In fact, no one present in that moment could believe what was **happening**.

Well, that's not strictly true.

Juba did.

The entire crowd had **frozen** in shock, but the Furleenian knew what to do immediately. He hit a button situated upon his belt. There were three such buttons and he often worried about pressing the wrong one.

On the right was a pulsar which fired percussive sound blasts. The middle one operated his rocket-pack which had been designed by Furleenian science-priests and enabled them to ascend (and then, should they choose, rain-flaming death upon their enemies).

The third button released him from his underwear, which

would be awkward, particularly in the heat of **battle**.

Luckily for him, he pressed the middle button and ascended to Tunde's floating position. He pressed 'translate' on his all-purpose communications device and spoke.

'You don't want to go back down there, do you?' he said. 'I don't blame you.'

Tunde felt as if he were in a dream. A dream in which he had just scored a **winning** goal and was now doing a post-match interview with a giant, flying ginger cat. He shook his head in disbelief.

'How are you **flying**?' he asked, bewildered. 'Are you a giant ginger cat? In fact, how am I flying?'

Juba sighed. Time on Earth had made the hatchling a little less quick-witted than might be hoped.

He replied with reasonable patience. 'I fly, hatchling, because of this —' and he indicated the rocket-pack under his cloak. He continued: 'And *you* fly because, as you can see, you are now the proud owner of your beautiful wings. Congratulations, by the way.'

Tunde nodded, still stunned. He'd never been complimented for having wings before, least of all by a ginormous ginger tom with a jet-pack.

This must be a dream, he thought. That was the only explanation; maybe Quinn had tackled him too hard and he had a concussion. He looked at the crowd below — they were all shielding their eyes, trying to figure out if this was some kind of ELABORATE magic trick.

The flying cat started talking again.

'My name is Juba. I come in peace. We must leave now. I have someone you need to meet.'

Tunde shook his head, trying to clear it. 'Do you know me?'

'Of course,' said Juba. 'I have been seeking you for a long time.'

Juba scanned the crowd. They were all taking out **COMMUNICATION** devices to record or photograph the phenomenon of the boy with wings. There wasn't much time.

Juba hit himself in the chest three times, hard, and screamed with all his might.

The noise was akin to that of fingernails down a blackboard, or a dozen cats being dropped into an ice bath simultaneously. Or the last British Eurovision Song Contest entry.

EEEEEEEEEEEEAAAAAAAEEEEEEEEEEE-AAAAAAAEEEEEEAAAAAAEEEEEEEEEAAAAA!

Everyone in the crowd clasped their ears and made a face as if to say, 'Please turn this off. I promise I'll be good for the rest of my life.'

Juba nodded, satisfied. He patted Tunde three times on the chest and an amazing thing happened. Tunde's wings folded away under his skin, smooth as butter. Juba **grabbed** him and they floated back down to the ground.

And, as everyone stared upwards into the space where a boy with **wings** and a giant, rocket-propelled moggie had just been, Juba speed-walked Tunde away from the football ground.

The second they were gone, everybody in the crowd shook their heads and wondered why they'd been **holding** their ears. They all looked expectantly at the pitch. Some of them were sure something had just happened. They just weren't sure what.

Nev, Jiah and Kylie frowned at each other.

Nev spoke first. 'That really hurt my ears,' he said.

'What happened?' asked Jiah.

'I think something **loud** happened . . . but I can't quite remember,' said Kylie thoughtfully. And then she looked at the pitch. The referee was about to **BLOW** her **whistle** again for extra time.

Jiah said, 'Where's Tunde?'

Nev looked out at the pitch **quickly**. 'He's gone.'

Kylie said, 'Where? He was here a minute ago.'

Quinn Patterson whooped and laughed at them from the touchline.

'Your mate's run off!' he **jeered**. 'All them goals was lucky

flukes. Now it's time for you to watch a real footballer in action.' And he jumped back to the centre spot.

Dembe ran over to the halfway line. 'Where is he?' she called.

Nev shook his head. 'No idea,' he said, frowning. 'But I think something's wrong. He would never abandon the game.'

Jiah made a **decision**. 'We should go to his house – if something's happened, that's where he'll be.'

And she set off immediately, because Jiah didn't *mess* about. Kylie followed, shifting her chair into (what she thought of as) 'warp speed'. Nev trotted along behind, thankful that his ankle had mostly recovered. To his surprise, Dembe followed too.

He **glanced** at her and she shrugged. 'Tunde's never missed a practice and he wouldn't miss the end of this game for the world,' she said. 'Something's up.'

Quinn Patterson yelled from the pitch. 'Where you goin'? The game's not over!'

But Dembe didn't even look back. Somehow this seemed much, much more important. Tunde was gone – and she and everyone else wanted to know why . . .

8
MUM?

As Tunde and Juba approached St Pritchett's Park, they soon found themselves under the canopy of a verdant forested area.

'Here we are,' said Juba, looking around. 'Tap your chest three times.'

'Why?' said Tunde suspiciously. He still wasn't entirely sure this wasn't a hallucination.

'Just do it,' said Juba patiently. 'It's time you learned.'

Tunde rather hesitantly tapped his chest and his wings reappeared. **FWOOOOOOSH!**

He craned his neck to see them. They were magnificent. Wild and powerful. It was as though an argumentative eagle had landed on his back and just wouldn't let go.

'Are you ready?' said Juba.

'Ready for what?'

'To fly, of course.'

Tunde glanced up. There was a great deal of greenery overhead – an abundance of trees, bushes and branches, resembling an enormous green duvet.

'Keep low,' said Juba. 'Low and watchful. Just follow me.'

Juba took off smoothly. Following some sort of instinct, Tunde flapped his wings, and soared.

'Not too high,' called Juba. 'Keep beneath the trees. Humans are not ready to see this and I don't have the energy to wipe any more minds.'

'All right,' said Tunde, and just like that, he found himself lowering slightly. It felt completely natural. As natural to him as running or kicking a ball or leaping into the air to do a massive, match-winning header.

They set off. Tunde smiled in awe. This was ah-maz-ing! **'Wooooohooooooo!'** he yelled. 'I'm **flying**.'

Juba rocketed ahead, confidently following the directions on his translation device, which now operated as an **ULTRA-HIGH-TECH** Furleenian GPS system, displaying his whereabouts with pinpoint accuracy. Soon they had escaped the bounds of St Pritchett's Park and had entered the Great Forest.

Tunde and his friends were fortunate to live near here as it was 'An Area of Natural Beauty' – at least that's what the local council said. It was thick with trees, bushes and various types of wild flora; very much a British forest, but in summer, if you closed your eyes and poured a bucket of warm water over your head, it felt like you were in the Amazon jungle. There was so much greenery overhead, so many trees: English oaks, beech, willow, pine, ash. It was like being in Sir David Attenborough's allotment.

There were wild horses roaming the area, free of rider and saddle, jostling for position. They looked up and saw Tunde and Juba flying side by side, swooping and soaring, and they neighed and **whinnied** loudly, echoing their movement.

Tunde looked down and smiled, almost flying into a tree in the process.

Juba snapped, 'Pay attention!'

Tunde joyfully followed the large flying cat's instructions (like this was an everyday thing), navigating the forest with ease.

'I can't believe this,' he called to Juba. 'I thought it would take me ages to learn.'

Juba gave him a thoughtful look. 'It does, for most,' he said. 'But **clearly**, you are special.'

And as he led the boy through bower and bloom, over branches and winding streams, past green and pleasant scenery, a cheeky magpie joined them, squawking **encouragement**. Tunde was sure he understood what the bird was saying – it sort of felt like:

'Stay level, ride the airwaves, keep your eyes peeled, avoid **SLAMMING** into the branches – you'll learn, young 'un!'

'It's time to land,' Juba said. He pointed below, not to the mossy ground but to an enormous beech tree that swayed majestically in the breeze. 'There.'

'There, as in, on top of that tree?' Tunde said cockily. 'No problem.'

Juba landed daintily, but Tunde had been overconfident. The tree rushed up to meet him as he landed too fast, skidded nine metres on a slippery branch and then teetered on the edge, above a twenty-metre drop to the rocky forest floor.

A strong hand **gripped** his wrist and yanked him upright as though he weighed no more than a starling.

Startled, Tunde looked up to see his saviour. And he found himself looking into a face almost exactly like his own – except this face belonged to a female, someone much, much taller than him. She was at least six feet tall and *magnificent* in appearance. Astounding, even.

She wore headwear that shone gold in the sunlight: not a crown or a helmet exactly, but something in between that shimmered and glowed as she turned her head. She wore a form-fitting suit with metallic highlights and her wings were huge, at least three times the size of Tunde's.

The bird-woman patted the top of her chest three times and her wings **VANISHED** from view.

She took him in from top to toe and said, 'At last. I am so honoured to meet you. For I am your mother.'

'Mother?' Tunde whispered.

'Yes. You were hatched from my egg.'

Tunde had to sit down **abruptly**. He'd just been told that he'd been hatched from an egg – that kind of thing doesn't happen every day.

His birth mother crouched next to him and said, 'We do not have time for sadness or confusion. There are things to do. You must wear your royal garments.'

She handed him a suit that was similar to hers and discreetly turned her back. Tunde undressed down to his pants, then stepped into it. For a moment he felt strange, prickly, as though his skin were being jabbed with hundreds of tiny needles, and then it didn't feel strange at all. It felt like the suit was made for him; it moulded to his body as comfortably as the comfiest tracksuit.

He glanced down at the suit.

There appeared to be weapons attached to it.

His wings, unbidden, suddenly extended to full width, wild and free.

Juba nodded and smiled. When he spoke, his voice was heavy with emotion. 'At last. You look extraordinary.'

His birth mother nodded in agreement. 'Yes, he does. Come. Let us go.'

Tunde was about to ask where exactly they were going, but before he could utter a word, his birth mother (his mother!) took to the skies boldly, beautifully, brilliantly. She soared, as if gravity were a joke. Her wings **pounded** the air beneath her as she slipped past the laws of nature and, with impressive ease, winged her way ever higher into the sky.

Tunde followed suit, and strangely, instinctively, knew exactly what to do and when to do it. As she ducked under a branch he would copy her; when he weaved, she would dive, and so on. When she broke free of the canopy and jetted a thousand feet in the air and then performed a magnificent power dive back towards the green, Tunde mimicked her movements without fear; and as he performed these aerial miracles without even a second thought – a brightly lit neon sign appeared in his mind's eye and it said simply:

I WAS BORN TO DO THIS.

And as he twisted his body with casual finesse and ascended into the clouds, he knew this statement was true.

In the same way that he was born to run and jump and

play football, he was also born to soar, swoop and skyrocket to the moon and back. And (his mind grew even more fevered as he pieced these notions together) this was better than the most exciting goal, the fastest race, the longest jump . . . Flying with your own wings was genius!

And his birth mother was training him, giving him a crash course in flight, aerodynamics, evasive action. But it didn't actually feel like teaching, not exactly; it was more like she was reminding him of what he already knew he could do. Of what he was capable of achieving.

'I can't believe I'm doing this!' he called out.

She glanced at him, surprised. 'Of course you are doing this,' she said. 'It is your birth right. I am simply JOGGING your instinctive memory.'

As he flapped and twisted and tucked, Tunde considered his instinctive memory well and truly jogged.

They found themselves once more at the enormous beech tree. Tunde performed an almost perfect landing this time, arriving on the thickest branch with the merest hint of a wobble; his wings provided a counterbalance, and he was able to style it out.

His birth mother nodded her approval.

'Good. You have done well, as I expected. You are prepared now for the task ahead – almost.'

Tunde stared at her.

'Task? What task? What am I supposed to be doing?'

His mother cocked her head, like an inquisitive sparrow, her eyes shining with a smile, and said:

'I will **tell you what you need to know**, and no more. You and I are from the planet Aviaan. For reasons that I will explain, you were hatched here on Earth. The citizens of Aviaan call me Aan. I am **PARTNERED** with the Supreme Leader, Aaven. I believe he has been captured and is being held **prisoner**. We must rescue him.'

Tunde said, 'Wait, wait, wait. Hang on, rescue him? Rescue *who*? I can't rescue anyone! I've got maths homework!'

His birth mother nodded patiently. 'It is a lot for you to take in, I understand this. But we do not have much time to spare. The Supreme Leader is in danger. And we must—'

Tunde cut across her and let words burble from his mouth without even thinking about it.

'Why's it down to me to rescue the Supreme Leader? I'm only twelve!'

She looked at him sharply.

'Do not **INTERRUPT** me. I am your elder. You will respect me or risk consequences.'

Tunde nodded. Fair enough, he thought. He knew that Ruth and Ron would have questions, though. To say the least.

'Who is this Supreme Leader?' he asked, in a quieter voice. 'The Supreme Leader of what?'

'Of our planet, of course. His survival is vital to our own. He is also, incidentally, my partner and your birth father. The one with whom I connected before you were hatched.'

'My birth father,' breathed Tunde. This was almost too much for his boyish brain. There were so many things to think about – his birth mother, his birth father, the planet Aviaan, an alien space suit, wings (of course), and a giant flying cat – and so he stopped thinking about them (otherwise his mind would turn into mush) and just accepted the situation.

'You say my father, the, er, Supreme Leader, is being held captive. Do you know where?'

Juba flipped a switch on his translator.

'He is being held at an Earth-based science complex nearby called Global SciTech, known by the locals as The Facility.'

Tunde **SWALLOWED**. He said in a small voice, 'My mum and dad work there.'

Juba ignored him and continued:

'The Supreme Leader has been held prisoner there for twelve Earth years. The time has finally arrived. You have become your true self, hatchling. You will assist us in stopping the battle.'

'Battle? What d'you mean, battle?' Tunde didn't like the sound of that. 'I'm rubbish at fighting. I don't want to fight anyone.'

Aan looked at him in disbelief.

'Is this the true son of Aaven and Aan?' she said in a **low** voice. 'What is this simpering cowardice? We have battled the Furleenians for aeons. Countless lives have been lost to the cause. But I am not asking you to *join* a war – I am asking you to help me end it.'

'To end it?' said Tunde.

She **nodded**. 'Yes. For this ancient and unending struggle to cease, I need you by our side. You must convince the Supreme Leader that this warring has cost far too many lives for no real **reward**. Juba, the Furleenian . . .'

She glanced at Juba, who nodded, grateful to get a mention (and to be appreciated; after all, he had been working very hard).

Aan continued:

'Juba, the Furleenian, has been in constant talks with

interested parties from both sides who are keen to stop the war. But unless your father agrees, such efforts will fail. And there is only one to whom he will **LISTEN**. The Son Foreseen.'

'You mean, he won't listen to you?' said Tunde.

Aan gave the slightest scowl. 'From past experience, no, he will not listen to me.'

Tunde shook his head. 'I've got to talk to my parents before I agree to any of this. I bet they're getting worried.'

Aan **frowned again**. 'I am your mother – you are my hatchling. The Supreme Leader gave you life!'

Surprising himself with the quickness of his reply, Tunde snapped back:

'Yes, but my adopted parents have looked after me and loved me and encouraged me and done homework with me . . . and everything else, for the last twelve years while you lot were off fighting your endless war. We need to let them know that I haven't been **kidnapped** by weirdos in a van or something. And I think you should meet them. Please?'

The minute he said it he regretted it, then wondered how Aviaans punished their young.

His mind worked quickly and then he added, 'If you don't, people might start looking for me and then there'll be a lot of fuss.'

Juba nodded.

'This is wise. We must attend to the adoptive parents. We can always make sure they have no memory of this.'

Aan sighed, then nodded her agreement.

Tunde was very relieved. Aan extended her magnificent

wings and took to the sky. Tunde echoed her every move, **zoomed off** and even overtook her as they roared off at speed into the grey-blue skies above. Within moments, they were riding the airwaves several hundred feet above Tunde's house.

While Tunde was being reunited with his Aviaan birth mother, and undergoing flight training over and above the Great Forest, Jiah, Kylie, Nev and Dembe (still in her football kit) made their way via the 472 bus and then on to Tunde's house.

Dembe **banged on the door** impatiently.

'Round here,' called Ron.

Tunde's dad was in the garden. He had called in sick to work that day and had been weeding and grumbling and muttering about how they didn't appreciate him or Ruth and they could all go and boil their heads – he mumbled these things as he tended a new variety of more muscular sweet pea.

As they came into view, he was genuinely **surprised** to see them.

'What are you all doing here?' he asked, looking at them and **GRINNING**. 'Wait. Where's Tunde?'

Nev spoke for everybody. 'We don't know. We thought he'd come home.'

The smile faded from Ron's face. 'What do you mean – he isn't at school? When did you last see him?' His gaze landed on Dembe and he pointed. 'And who are you?'

'I'm Dembe Diallo, I'm on the same football team as Tunde. He disappeared at the end of the match. By the way, at my last school, the headteacher said it was rude to randomly point at people.'

Ron politely **lowered** the offending digit.

'Football team?' he said. 'What do you mean, football team?'

Dembe looked puzzled. 'Er. They're a b-i-i-g part of the game *football*? You know? The players wear shorts, boots, a top, sometimes they have mad hair. They're always takin' a knee. You've probably seen it on television.'

Ron shook his head. 'I don't need to be cheeked by you, young lady. My son was specifically told not to **PLAY** *any* sports.'

Nev said, 'Yeah, I heard 'bout that. I thought you was being a **bit mean**, to be honest. Tunde's got basically astonishing skills, yeah? Now he's just . . . gone all Bermuda triangle an' that. We thought he'd be here.'

Ron shook his head. 'No, he isn't. Look, wait here, will you?' He ran inside the house and a **second later** he was back with Ruth.

'What do you mean, Tunde's gone? Is this some sort of game?' She took one look at their worried and confused faces. 'You'd better come in.'

They marched in. Ruth pointed to Dembe. 'Boots at the door please.'

Dembe pulled a face behind Ruth's back, but still did as she'd been asked. The others had already removed their shoes

123

and Kylie checked her wheels for mud. They knew the rules in the Wilkinson house.

They all sat down in the front room whilst Ron spoke in hushed tones on the phone in the hallway.

Ruth paced around nervously. 'Cup of tea?' she said. 'Do you want some cake? **Don't worry**, it's just chocolate and ginger and stuff.'

At the word 'stuff' everybody hesitated as they remembered Ruth's seedy and nutty gloopy mutant birthday cake. Dembe, who was clueless about Ruth's baking skills, said, 'I'll have some.'

Ruth went to the door, but Nev caught Dembe's eye and **shook his head vigorously** like a Saint Bernard that had just been caught in a downpour.

'You do not want Ruth's cake,' he whispered. 'It'll be raw and full of mud and earth and insects and things.'

Dembe's eyes widened as she **YELLED** loudly, so Ruth could hear in the kitchen, 'Er, actually, d'you know what, Mrs Wilkinson? I'm not feelin' cake just now, yeah?'

There was a muffled 'OK' and then they heard cups and saucers rattling off in the distance.

Nev nodded, wiped his brow. **'Lucky escape.'**

Kylie gave her the thumbs up.

Jiah closed her eyes and raised a palm to the heavens.

Ruth **re-entered** and clocked all this but ignored them. 'Where do you think Tunde is?'

Kylie said, 'We don't know. It's like, one minute he was playing brilliantly and scoring goals, next minute, he's gone!'

Ruth chewed her lip. 'We told him not to play football,' she muttered. Then she yelled to Ron out the door. 'Any news?'

Ron shouted back, 'They're going to send someone.'

'Who's going to send who?' Jiah asked.

Ruth said, 'Just, ah . . . some people from work.'

Nev said, 'But don't you think you should call the five-o?'

Ruth shook her head. 'There's other people to talk to before we get to the police. Now, who wanted a cup of tea?'

Dembe caught Nev's eye, who caught Jiah's eye, who caught Kylie's. This was eye **eye catching** to an unbelievable level of skill. Through complex eye-based signals, everyone was basically saying: *Something ain't right.* For a start, Ron and Ruth weren't behaving like people who'd just heard their son had **disappeared**. What did 'other people to talk to before we get to the police' mean?

Jiah stood up.

'I'm sorry, Mrs Wilkinson, but you're **behaving** very strangely indeed. You offer us tea and inedible cake and say we don't need to tell the police. We, on the other hand, are very concerned about your son's well-being. We haven't seen Tunde since just before the full-time whistle – one minute he'd jumped up to head the ball, the next he was gone. We were **WATCHING** Tunde, and then – it's like he was never there.'

Dembe nodded excitedly. 'That's the thing. OK, we can't remember what happened – but he can't have just *disappeared*, can he? He would have gone somewhere? It wasn't a big enough gap for him to disappear completely. He should have been by the bus stop around the corner, by the sweet shop, or at least by the kebab cafe.'

Nev **nodded**. 'Yeah, fam, T wasn't gone that long.'

Kylie was on the verge of tears. 'So where is he?' She looked at Ruth. 'Don't you care?'

Ruth stared at her. 'Of course I care,' she said quietly. 'It's just—'

At that point, there was a light **tap tap tap** at the door. They all jumped.

Ron rushed over and flung the door open, and there stood Tunde.

Only, he didn't really look like Tunde. For a start he was dressed differently — in a glittering uniform. Like some sort of . . . **SUPERHERO**.

He looked more confident than anyone had ever seen.

'Mum, Dad,' he said. 'I've got somebody I want you to meet.'

Ruth snapped back in full-on Jamaican-Mum mode. 'Meet? How yu mean, "meet"? Get y'backside in this blouse-and-skirt house! Now! Where've you been? We've been worried sick.'

Tunde looked at his feet, encased in their gleaming, shimmering boots. 'Please, Mum,' he said quietly.

Ruth took a **deep breath** and said, in her 'Uh-oh, I just totally went full-on Jamaica-style in front of strangers, better chill' voice, 'Well, who are these people? Who exactly do you want us to meet?'

Tunde looked up and nodded.

And the next thing that happened was jaw-droppingly astonishing.

From high above the doorstep of Tunde's house, the sound of a purring rocket-pack, followed by gorgeous wingbeats, preceded Aan and Juba as they descended to and then **landed** on the Wilkinsons' front path as if their feet were encased in cotton wool. Perfection.

Aan's wings **DISAPPEARED** into her back coverings,

and she stood there regally, looking at Ruth, who was thunderstruck and speechless.

Ron was also flummoxed. (Right now, if there had been a place called Flummox-ville nearby, there would most definitely be a **HEAD-SCRATCHING** statue of Ron in the town centre.) He stared at his son. 'Do you want to explain why you look like you're auditioning to be in the school nativity play? And who are these –' he wanted to say 'nutters', but bit his tongue – 'people?'

Tunde said, 'Can we go in the house, please? Everyone's watching.'

Ruth stood to one side and allowed Juba, Aan and Tunde to walk past her and into the hallway. She **looked** out on to the street, just in case everyone *was* watching, but, strangely, there were no nosey neighbours peering from behind twitching net curtains . . . All seemed quiet. She shut the door firmly behind her.

In the front room, Tunde's reappearance was causing a commotion.

Nev looked at him. 'Oh my days. Dude! You look cooler than a polar bear wearing shades drivin' a Bentley, bruv!'

Jiah said, 'Where'd you get the weird outfit? Who's the big cat guy? Imagine his litter tray – that would take up the entire house!'

Kylie was **frightened**. 'Tunde, why d'you look so weird? One minute you're playing football, and the next minute you're dressed like a superhero back-up dancer! I'm having a panic attack.'

Tunde hesitated. He tried to say the next bit the best way he could. 'Everybody calm down, OK? I've been . . . Well, there's some things you lot don't know . . . about me. Things I've only just found out myself. I've got . . . Well, why don't I just –'

He tapped his chest three times, and **FWOOOOOOOOSH!**

His wings fully extended. They took up the entire front room, almost hitting Nev in the face.

There was a moment of stunned silence.

Then Jiah said, 'You have wings! Statistically impossible, but who cares! Oh my goodness. I need to make notes, take pictures! This should be in a scientific journal. Tunde! You have **WINGS!**'

Kylie said, 'Oh my gosh. They're beautiful! I'm having a moment.'

Dembe totally couldn't handle it. She was speechless. She'd never seen anything like this.

Ruth had tears in her eyes as she said, 'They did tell us – that something like this might happen around now. They warned us about you running around; said fast-paced motion might trigger it early – that's why we tried so hard to keep you from doing sports. I'm so sorry, son. We should've told you much earlier than this.'

Ron was crying too. 'You weren't ever meant to know. They said it was best that way . . .'

'What do you mean "they"?' said Tunde coldly. 'Are you talking about The Facility?'

Ruth and Ron **NODDED**. 'They – The Facility – suggested

129

we take you in. We didn't know how you'd come to be there but you were such a little thing – so tiny and lovely – we just wanted to protect you.'

Tunde looked at them. 'You knew about –' and he **pointed** to his wings. 'You knew about these?'

They both nodded.

Ruth took over. 'Well, not quite. They said you were different from other babies. But we weren't to ask any more questions.'

'Growing up on Earth would affect your development, and if we were careful you'd be able to blend in, but we always knew something like this might happen. Tunde, I want you to know that we love you very, very much, and we'll always be here for you.'

Tunde **shouted**. 'Always be here for me?! You knew I was going to sprout feathers when I was twelve? My birth parents are aliens . . . with wings! And you never said anything? What's the matter with you?'

Aan stepped forward; she'd heard enough. 'Tunde! Your elders are to be treated with respect at all times. They have done nothing but care for you. **Remember** this is a shock to everyone. It's not every day you discover your only child is an alien hatchling from another dimension.'

Ron stared at her. '*Another dimension?* What, like Wolverhampton?'

Ruth **glared** at him: *Really?*

But Ron carried on regardless:

'The Facility said he was *different*, but they didn't mention an alternate dimension, did they, Ruth?'

'Ah,' said Ruth, rather shiftily. 'No, not exactly.'

Ron **frowned**. 'Wait. What do you know?'

Ruth looked at everyone staring at her expectantly 'There was an . . . *event* at work, just before Tunde was born. We lost a few members of staff in a blow-up in the sub-sub-sub-basement. I know that shortly after this *event*, we were offered Tunde, no questions asked. We . . .'

And she cried now, almost from the bottom of her heart.

'We wanted a baby of our own so much . . .'

Aan looked at them with great understanding. 'You **took** our hatchling and raised him as your own – for that we thank you.'

She raised her hands to her head-covering and removed it, **revealing** an almost-human face – but with a light covering of jet-black feathers. Her nose, if you looked closely, was almost beak-like. Her ears were almost flat against her head, and her hair resembled Tunde's: light and feathery more than curly. She was otherworldly in **appearance**, but stunning. Like an African bird goddess.

Jiah couldn't help it. 'Tunde, your birth mum is a total bird-lady,' she said.

Nev gasped. 'I might have to sit down.'

Dembe nodded. 'This is the coolest thing I've ever seen in my whole life. Tunde. Your rellies are bird folk, man. Respeck!'

Tunde said, 'She says we have to rescue my birth father. The Supreme Leader. He's locked up in the sub-sub-sub-basement at The Facility.'

Ruth replied, 'Yeah. About that . . .'

'What? About what? Do you—'

But before Ruth could explain, they heard the sound of a dozen drumming boots pounding up the front path, and then **WHAMMO!**

The front door flew off its hinges!

Ron sighed. 'You could've just rung the doorbell!'

But no one listened to him. Everyone was staring at the hard-looking Facility staff members in **SWAT TEAM**-style helmets, gloves, visors and communications devices. All of them were armed with weird-looking weapons. One of them stepped forward and removed his helmet.

'Hello, everyone,' said Marcus Humphries, looking particularly smug. 'We're all going for a little drive to The Facility for a teensy chat. Transport's been laid on free of charge, so if you'd all step outside.'

Aan **looked** at him. 'I will make my own way.'

Humphries grinned humourlessly and said, 'No. We'd

rather like it if you *didn't* do that,' and a security operative **stepped forward**. Before anyone could speak, the room was filled with tranquillizer mist and everybody without a protective mask fainted away like an over-excited teen at a boy-band concert.

Moments later, the magpie (remember him from the Prologue?) zipped along thirty metres above the security transport as it headed towards The Facility. The bird had been perched on the Wilkinson window ledge, eavesdropping, and – *what larks*! He couldn't wait to tell the others: the boy had WINGS!

It watched as the Wilkinsons, some other children, a **very** bird-like woman (she **smelled** like a relative), and (what smelled like) a giant ginger feline, were herded into a van.

The magpie decided to follow.

Now it shook its head as it rocketed along, devouring odd flies and insects as they whipped into its open maw.

Eventually it nosedived and drew level with the windows, trying to peek inside as the vehicle sped along. It didn't catch much – although it could see the bird-woman bound and gagged in the back.

In The Facility transport, Ron and Ruth **rode up front**, hardly noticing the curious magpie flying alongside.

Tunde, Jiah, Dembe, Nev and Kylie were all strapped into their seats and were **bouncing** along, half asleep and dreaming.

Tunde's dream was about something bright and huge and star-like . . . something fierce and dangerous. It was a dream he'd had before . . . but he was having them more frequently now.

The magpie **beat its wings** and retook its place thirty metres above the truck as it arrived at The Facility. It wondered if the boy was in danger. For some reason, this place didn't give off a good vibe.

9

PLEASED TO MEET YOU

The Facility transport vehicle drove through a number of barriers, each one requiring voice recognition, an eyeball scan and a thumbprint.

The driver endured each of these interruptions to his journey with great patience, until the last two stops, by which time the sensation of having his eyeballs lasered multiple times had lost its charm. Not to mention his sore thumb, which pulsed as if it had been hit repeatedly with a cartoon polo mallet.

The driver blinked furiously, then headed down into the sub-sub-sub-basement of The Facility complex, where secret experiments occurred on a daily basis. This was the very place where the radioactive man bit a spider just to see what happened; where the inky-black lab-grown unicorn got the fifth-floor corner office with the nice view because who there would tell her no?

Now fully recovered from the tranquillizer mist and released from their bindings, they were marched into The Facility.

Emil Krauss stepped out of the shadows and examined them all with great interest.

He acknowledged that Aan was with them, also Juba, and nodded to them gracefully without a single hesitation or **EXCLAMATION** such as – 'Hang on, she looks just like Oprah Winfrey with feathers!' or 'That, right there, is a man-sized ginger cat!' Emil was cool and collected.

Tunde knew instinctively, immediately, that Emil was the man in charge and wanted to ask a gazillion intelligent questions – he had been chosen to stop an interdimensional war, after all – but instead he opted for: 'Who are you? What do you want?'

Emil smiled warmly. 'Tunde. I haven't seen you since you were an egg. My name is Emil Krauss, and I am, perhaps, the reason for all of this.'

Tunde waited. Aan and Juba were silent. The rest of the kids ~~tried~~ not to get too distracted by the fact they were in what amounted to a Bond villain's hideout, and all paid attention.

Emil glanced behind them.

'Ah, Marcus – you've **arrived**. Tunde, please meet my number two, Marcus Humphries. You've already met, of course – but let me formally introduce you.'

Marcus Humphries was standing in the doorway, with a tight smile on his lips and humourless eyes.

'Marcus Humphries, meet Tunde Wilkinson. You know him of old.'

Marcus smiled even harder and chose not to speak. Emil continued.

'Ruth, Ron – it's nice to see you. You should be very proud

of your parents, Tunde – your adoptive parents, I should say. Your mother runs the game theory and digital technology department, she's crucial to our organization. And your father's in genetics and such, isn't that right?'

Ron nodded.

'Yes – very **encouraging** work,' added Emil.

Ruth nodded slowly, but Ron couldn't believe it. He hadn't had a compliment from anyone at The Facility in twenty years.

Emil went on. 'When you **hatched** from your, quite frankly, rather large egg, Tunde, I imagined you'd need considerable help if you were going to live amongst us. We could have kept you hidden here at The Facility, but that seemed rather cruel. No, my idea was that you should hide in plain sight and be raised for the exact purpose for which you were brought here.'

Tunde licked his lips. 'Which is?'

Emil Krauss sighed. 'Your birth family and their enemies have been at war constantly for centuries. I am devoted to peace. For all of us, wherever we are from, whoever we are. I have **experienced** war first hand and have lost loved ones. Constant war is toxic, a disease, and should be stopped as best we can. I decided that the only way for Aviaans and Furleenians to learn about peace was for you, Tunde, to grow up amongst humans. To learn about compromise and to live in a flawed society. To have parents who **loved** you and wanted nothing more than for you to be kind and healthy. And so we made it possible for you to fit in.'

Tunde shook his head. 'I don't understand what you mean . . .'

'Well, look at you, Tunde. You're Black with curly hair and a beaky nose. You also have wings.'

Nev **interrupted and blurted**, 'Bruv, you went to a school where there was hardly anybody that looked like us anyway. Can you imagine what it would've been like if you'd had your wings out during games?'

Jiah laughed. 'I don't know. It would've helped in basketball.'

'But how can I help?' Tunde said.

Emil simply said, 'Do you want to meet your birth father? He's downstairs.'

And with that, he headed towards the lifts nearby. EVERYONE followed, Marcus Humphries bringing up the rear.

In the sub-sub-sub-basement there were security cameras bristling from almost every surface, every nook, cranny and corner. Krauss spoke softly into a walkie-talkie. 'Deactivate all cameras please.'

Suddenly every single CCTV camera whirled, whizzed, wobbled, and then collapsed and faced downwards like squiffy uncles at a barbecue.

Krauss spoke into his communication device once more. 'Release the doors please.'

And then two mammoth doors clicked, clacked, shunked and then whizzed back on rollers – **SHNNNNNNNNN-NNZZZZZZZZZZZZZZZZZZZZZ!**

As the doors opened wide, they saw a silhouette poised, as though ready to make its entrance.

Aaven stepped forward into the light; humanoid-shaped and over seven feet tall, with an almost beak-like nose and

eyes slightly further apart than most **HUMANS**, his skin was black and he had jet-black feathery hair just like Aan's, and a little like Tunde's.

Dembe couldn't believe her eyes. 'That's Tunde's birth father, and look! Look at his nose! Look at his eyes! They're definitely his mum and dad, innit?'

Tunde was **ASTOUNDED** and completely freaked out. His birth mother and father were there in front of him. He looked at Ron and Ruth for reassurance and they smiled encouragingly.

Tunde turned to Krauss. 'Why was he locked up in your sub-sub-sub-basement?'

Krauss said, 'Perhaps you'd like to speak to him first. Go on.'

Slowly Tunde walked towards his birth father.

He stepped into the cell. It was warehouse-sized – an enormous space, specifically designed for large flying creatures of humanoid size and shape.

There was more than enough room for Aaven to stretch his wings, and plenty of space and things to balance on. It reminded Tunde of an enormous budgie cage.

Tunde said, 'They shouldn't have done this to you.'

Aaven just looked at him. 'You are the hatchling. We are of the same blood.'

Tunde nodded and sniffed. He realized that he was crying.

'May I see your wings?' his father asked.

Tunde tapped his chest three times, like he'd been taught. His wings shot out. **FWOOOOOOSH!**

His birth father walked around him, examining the wings. 'Perfect,' he murmured. 'Better than I could have imagined.'

Tunde felt a glow of pride.

'Please,' his birth father said. 'Show me how you fly.'

Tunde **TOOK OFF** and flew around the space for a moment, navigating all the little obstacles that had been placed there for Aaven's exercise. Aaven joined him and suddenly there they were, father and son, winging their way through circular obstacles, over and under bars, and around upright slalom poles. Aaven laughed as they touched down.

'You are strong, powerful and impressive, my son.'

'Thanks . . . Father.' And Tunde went in for a hug, but Aaven **GRIPPED** him by the shoulders and looked him in the eyes.

He whistled then, a low tune, and, like a chord sequence unlocking and sounding in his mind, Tunde understood everything.

His birth father communicated in the Aviaan tongue: 'I have planned for this moment over these many seasons. Our first task is to escape this place, then we wage war on these Earthers and destroy them, locate the **escape craft**, make the jump back to our territories and extinguish the Furleenians once and for all. We will take back all spoils of war that are rightfully ours. You will reign by my side, and eventually lead us to even greater glory.'

Tunde was winded. He took a moment to absorb what he'd just been told, then, rather carefully, he asked: 'And then we just carry on **fighting wars** and that forever and ever?'

'Correct.'

Aaven clicked and whistled his approval.

Tunde looked beyond the cell's doors and said, 'I think **you and Mum** need to have a chat.'

The Supreme Leader looked at him and said, 'Mum? What is Mum?'

10
THE CONSULTATION

Tunde was beginning to regret this.

Aan and Aaven had been, let's say, *having a spirited discussion* for the best part of ninety minutes. Because of Juba's translator, the kids could understand every word of the **argument**, and after a while they began to wish they couldn't.

Aan had dominated proceedings for quite some time.

'. . . It's all about you, isn't it? With all your fancy plans about lording it over the Furleenians and having your own way, all the time. Not a thought about me. I'm just expected to . . . to . . . to **pop out eggs** one after the other, in the hope that you'll get a male heir just like you, who wants to keep fighting and fighting and fighting and – and I'm so tired, Aaven.'

Aaven met her gaze. 'I think you need to understand that **our reason** for being in this life *is* to war on the Furleenians, and indeed any other race, who would **DARE TO STEAL** our legacy from us? That is our sole reason for existence. To protect our legacy.'

Aan glared at him and shrugged her shoulders. Her feathers rippled as she shot back:

'What legacy? All the legacy we had was destroyed beyond all recognition. Where we live is wasteland. When we fly, we fly over ruination. We're at war all the time – either attacking or being attacked. It's been going on for far too long.'

She cleared her throat. 'And so, I've initiated a change.'

She glanced at Emil Krauss, who nodded.

Aaven flicked his head to one side and ruffled his feathers. 'What change?' he said. 'What have you done?'

Aan preened momentarily. 'Juba, the Furleenian diplomat . . . He and I have been talking.'

Aaven blinked his bright eyes. 'You have been talking to a Furleenian? About what?'

His head moved back and forth like a rooster who'd had too much coffee.

Aan looked at him and spoke very slowly and clearly, so there was no mistaking her words.

'Since the day you disappeared with our hatchling, I have pursued a peaceful way forward.'

Aaven snorted. 'A ridiculous idea.'

'I am not alone in this, Aaven. All the Aviaan females think peace is the only way for us all to continue, and the Furleenian females feel the same.'

Kylie, Jiah and Dembe looked at each other. Dembe HISSED, 'Girl power!'

Ruth shushed her, tugged her ear and whispered, 'Listen!'

Aan continued, determined to be heard.

'We and the Furleenian female contingent have drawn up

a plan that, when signed by the Supreme Leaders of both planets, will mean peace forever for all of us. We can help each other **rebuild**, start again. Live together, all of us, at last.'

The Supreme Leader roared and let forth a barrage of whistles, which Tunde understood to mean 'Never!' and 'Over my dead body!' and that he'd rather fly into a black hole first.

Behind them, Marcus surreptitiously tried to record everything with his camera phone, but Emil *put his hand* over the lens. 'Show some respect,' he whispered.

Marcus looked grumpy.

The argument continued. Aan circled her partner, her mighty wings twitching as her anger rose at every revolution.

'Have you learned nothing? We are almost on the verge of peace, Aaven, and still you would destroy everyone and everything rather than accept change. What's the matter with you? Don't you—'

Aaven **INTERRUPTED**. 'Beak and claw! I'm the Supreme Leader. Waging war is what we've always done. The hatchling needed to be under my protection. He's the Son Foreseen! They may have destroyed him otherwise.'

He extended his wings to their full breadth and flapped them aggressively. Everyone got caught in the backdraught.

'This is like a really **boring** tennis match,' said Tunde with a sigh. 'One that goes on forever and no one wins.'

'It's like my mum always says about couples therapy . . .' Kylie said, and then yelped. 'That's it!'

'What?' said Tunde.

'My mum told me about this,' Kylie said, her eyes shining.

'It happens when she's counselling couples. They become entrenched. Neither one wants to move because they're scared to fail, so they stick.'

Juba had his TRANSLATOR pointed at Kylie. He was interested.

'Kylie – I can't bring your mum here – she'd lose her mind. I'm the son of an alien couple and they're having a row that could end in my birth dad destroying our world and everyone in it. Anyway –' he gestured at Krauss and Humphries – 'they'd never let us do it.'

'They need to talk to someone, if they really *do* want peace. I'm telling you, my mum does this **every day**, she's written books about it – she'd know exactly how to deal with this.'

Nev nodded. 'Actually, that's a good shout, bruv . . .'

Jiah agreed. 'Anything's better than this – this is going on longer than the *Lord of the Rings* trilogy.'

Tunde stepped forward to where Aaven and Aan were still arguing furiously.

'Excuse me,' he said loudly. 'My friend Kylie understands what you are going through, and could perhaps help you find a solution that might satisfy both of you. It's called a . . . a compromise.'

The Supreme Leader glared at him imperiously. 'He is little more than a hatchling, he knows nothing. We need to return to our world and prepare for war.'

Aan exploded, 'War war war war war war war! **Blahblahblahblahblahblahblah!** Do you hear yourself?'

Aaven was so unused to being spoken to like this, he stopped and stared, speechless.

Aan looked at him and nodded. 'He's always been like this. It's always got to be his way or no way at all.'

Tunde **LOOKED** at his birth mother and father. 'Kylie's mother is a special therapist who works with couples who have some unresolved issues. And I think we need her now.'

'Oi, you're not dragging my mum into The Facility,' said Kylie. 'She works in her office or not at all.'

Dembe nodded and said, 'You two need to find another way to communicate, man, cos this in't working.'

Emil looked at Marcus. 'Well?'

Marcus replied smoothly. 'We could use Facility transport to make the journey, make it financially viable for her mother to talk to them: perhaps there will be a positive outcome. Of course, they *could* rip her to shreds with their beaks if they didn't like what she was **saying** . . . but it's a risk worth taking.'

Tunde watched Marcus as he spoke, and as he **did** so he realized something. In spite of the big smile and smooth voice, he totally understood at that moment that *he didn't trust Marcus at all.*

Meanwhile, Krauss spoke into his walkie-talkie, and soon a **Facility transport** vehicle was ready for them upstairs.

'Um, don't you want my address?' asked Kylie.

Marcus laughed. 'Don't worry about that,' he said. He smiled, showing all his teeth. 'We have our ways.'

They drove quickly through the streets. Unbeknownst to

them, they were followed by a string of inquisitive magpies.

Soon, the vehicle pulled up a few yards from Kylie's house. Kylie said to all of them, 'Let me go in first. I don't want to freak my mum out. She's really sensitive. I'll need to explain it to her very gently. She might have to light a candle and meditate for this much stress.'

They **lowered** the ramp and she sped down to the door of her house. She knocked and her mum answered. She was wearing an orange blouse, floaty skirt and pointy shoes. A scarf was tied round her head and she had purple eye make-up on.

'Kylie! What are you doing home from school? I **THOUGHT** there was a football match.'

Jiah had to stop herself from laughing; she turned to Dembe and whispered, 'Kylie's mum dresses like one of my aunties!'

Kylie ignored her and said, 'Mum, I need your help.'

'I'm in the middle of work, love. **In fact**, I'm mid-session, on the verge of a breakthrough.'

'You're going to have to tell them to go.'

'Tell them to go? They're my clients, Kylie – plus, they've paid for this session. I can't—'

Suddenly Marcus **appeared** at Kylie's side. He oozed charm. 'I'm so sorry to interrupt, Mrs Collins. We have some new clients for you, but it really is very urgent you meet. In terms of the financial aspect, I think this might take care of things,' he said, and he handed her an envelope.

Kylie's mum opened it and saw a roll of fifty-pound

notes that would choke a Brontosaurus. She turned on her heel immediately and went back in the house; the next thing everyone saw was a **bedraggled**, tear-sodden couple, both clutching boxes of tissues, being hustled out the door by Kylie's mum as she told them, 'Terrific progress, really wonderful, see you next week. You can keep the tissues.'

She shoved them both out of the door and turned to face Kylie and the others, who emerged from the truck.

'Now, what do you need me to do?'

Marcus nodded to Krauss, who gave a signal, and Aaven and Aan *glided over* and landed on the front doorstep.

Juba walked up, pulled down his hood, revealed his whiskery, furry face and spoke. 'We understand you are a negotiator of the highest standard. We require your assistance.'

Kylie's mum looked at the three creatures, then fainted with a loud **THUMP!**

'Uh-oh,' said Kylie. 'I told you she was sensitive.'

While Kylie was reviving her mum, Emil Krauss's phone rang. He stepped aside, spoke for a few minutes, and then hung up. Tunde noticed that his expression was thunderous.

'Marcus,' he said. 'Can I speak to you for a moment?'

While the two men went off to talk, Kylie's mum sat up and **blinked** at the alien creatures.

'Are these . . . ?'

'Your new clients? Yes they are, Mum.'

Everyone sat waiting outside the treatment room as the therapy session took place inside. They could hear voices

being raised and the low, soothing
murmur of Kylie's mum.

They heard Aan say, 'We're on the verge of
peace. All you have to do is give this your approval
and we can start again.'

Then they heard Kylie's mum speaking quietly, then the

Supreme Leader said, 'I now have the talking stick. What good is peace? They'll only attack again, why should they **change?'**

Juba nodded. This was true.

Then he saw something on a nearby shelf. He waved the translator over it. It was a book called *If You Love Me, Let Me Win Sometimes: Relationship Hacks for Busy Couples*, by Lisa Collins.

There was a photoshopped picture of Kylie's mum on the cover in two different outfits arguing with herself.

Juba began scanning it with his translator, nodding vigorously from time to time. Dembe watched him.

'You readin' that?' Dembe said.

'No. I am absorbing it.'

Kylie said, 'Take one. Take half a dozen! There are crates of them in the garage gathering dust.'

Juba nodded thoughtfully and continued scanning.

After about an hour, the door opened. Kylie's mum **POKED** her head out and smiled in triumph.

'I think,' she whispered, 'that we might have made some progress here today.'

She **opened** the door a little wider and allowed the couple to re-emerge.

Carrying a small stick, the Supreme Leader led Aan out of the room saying, 'I have been a fool. I have not listened to you. I care for you.'

Aan took the stick from him and **REPLIED**:

'At least you have tried to listen to my point of view. I am in favour of this new Aaven. Perhaps we can find peace in this way and move forward.'

Aaven retrieved the stick and nodded vigorously.

'I feel like I have wasted so much time.'

Juba stood. 'There are many useful things in this human book that will help in our peace process.'

The Supreme Leader nodded. He stroked Aan's back and feathers and said, 'I care for you deeply.'

Aan **looked** at him and said, 'Hmm. Don't overdo that.'

Krauss appeared in the doorway. 'Hello, everyone.'

'Great news,' said Tunde. 'We think my birth mum and dad have agreed to compromise.'

Krauss nodded. 'That is great news. However, Earth is about to be attacked. Furleenian warships have just entered through the dimensional rip and are on the outskirts of our atmosphere.'

Juba nodded wearily and glanced back at the book. 'They are locked in a repeating pattern of never-ending behaviour. It's textbook. Lisa Collins has much to say on this in Chapter Nine—'

The Supreme Leader interrupted him.

'We must take our ship and **see** if we can dissuade this rogue breakaway group from this path of further war. Perhaps we could take the talking stick.'

Aan said, 'Not without me you won't.'

And Tunde said, 'I want to come with you.'

Then Dembe, Kylie, Jiah and Nev all **nodded** vigorously. Kylie spoke for everyone else when she said, 'We're not letting you go anywhere without us.'

Ron and Ruth looked at the youngsters with pride.

Krauss smiled. 'You are all very brave. All right, everyone, back to the transport.'

They all filed out. Juba hung back and held his paw out formally to Kylie's mum.

'You are wise, and you have perhaps saved two races from tearing each other to shreds in further war. Many thanks from all of us.'

He took her by the hand and licked it. Juba pulled the door closed and heard a loud **THUMP** on the other side. Kylie's mum had fainted again.

They drove back to The Facility at speed, Krauss waved them past all security via walkie-talkie, and they were back at the sub-sub-sub-basement lab in minutes.

'Down here,' said Emil Krauss, sprinting as though he wasn't over a hundred years old.

They **hurried** to the Portal Room.

'Wow,' said Tunde as he **stepped** through the door, eyeing the enormous ship. He had imagined spaceships before of course – but in his wildest dreams, he had never thought he would see one.

As the Supreme Leader entered the enormous lab space, the ship **raised** itself and hovered, almost expectantly.

'It's moving,' said Marcus, his eyes shining with excitement. 'We've been trying to get it to do something like this for years.'

The Supreme Leader shrugged. 'It only responds to Aviaan

vibrations – or approved alternate vibrations.'

Jiah said, 'You mean like DNA?'

Nev nudged her. 'Why are you talking to the big bird-man? Don't. He's scary.'

Jiah said, 'He's interesting. I'm interested. Why wouldn't I talk to him? Honestly, **you're being a wuss**. I'm a scientist and this is more exciting than double maths and physics.'

Aaven explained further:

'It only responds to the Aviaan vibrations or anybody that is *of* our people or *with* our people. It operates through our minds and not through physical movement.'

The doors of the ship zizzed open and revealed a super-clean glowing interior.

A familiar voice said, 'Sentient Hyper-Intelligent Pan-Planetary Entity **ready** for boarding. Would you like to play, Tunde?'

Aaven looked sternly at his birth child. 'Hatchling, have you been playing with this ship?'

Tunde looked at him shyly. 'Erm . . . I don't really understand – but I think my mum might have . . .'

Ruth stepped forward. 'We thought it might be important that Tunde get acquainted with the technology. I've been working on an interface for years, trying to work out how it functions. We had no joy until the kids began playing it like a game. S.H.I.P.P.E. responded to them, it knows them.'

Aaven nodded gravely. 'Thank you,' he said, 'for preparing our hatchling.'

Ruth nodded. 'Good luck with your peace mission.'

Marcus stepped forward too. 'I'm coming with you.'

Krauss intervened. 'That's not a good idea, Marcus. This is not our affair. We have interfered once in the name of peace, but now we must step aside.'

Marcus's face clouded over and he said, 'I've been waiting for this for over twelve years. Ever since this thing arrived, I knew that one day I would take a ride in it!'

Krauss looked at him. 'Marcus, these beings have also been waiting a long time for this. They are suing for peace and we must respect that.'

Tunde said, 'Let him come with us. We can handle him. S.H.I.P.P.E. – Marcus Humphries is with us, yeah?'

S.H.I.P.P.E. replied, 'Absolutely, Captain Tunde, shall we initiate take-off?'

Marcus strolled into the body of S.H.I.P.P.E. as though he were about to buy a second-hand car.

Tunde said, 'Dembe, you next. S.H.I.P.P.E. needs to scan you – it's part of the game.'

S.H.I.P.P.E. made a noise as Dembe walked through the entrance.

'Ah yes, Dembe Diallo, you are **CLEARED** for take-off.'

And then S.H.I.P.P.E spoke in a kind of South-Central LA voice and said: 'Now where the rest of my girls at?'

Kylie and Jiah rocked up to the entrance.

'Same set-up for me, yeah, S.H.I.P.P.E?' Kylie said excitedly.

'Absolutely,' S.H.I.P.P.E. replied. 'And Jiah, your display is just as you left it – I know you don't like mess.'

'Thank you, S.H.I.P.P.E.,' said Jiah calmly. 'Commence

calculating distance and time to this dimensional rip. We're up and almost ready for departure.'

The Supreme Leader, Aan and Juba took their positions within the womb of the craft. Then the rest sat or stood as if they'd been doing this all their lives.

It was just as if they were playing the S.H.I.P.P.E. Space Fighter game; Nev, Jiah, Kylie and Tunde all put goggles on and attached rope-like bands to their wrists. Suddenly the ship vroomed into pre-take-off mode.

Lights shifted from gold, to red, to amber, and finally to green; Marcus looked around in wonder. He sat and strapped himself in. No rope-like control bands **appeared** for him.

'Hey,' he said. 'Where are my controls?'

Tunde glanced at him.

'You're here to observe. We're in charge now.'

Marcus scowled. The entrance closed.

Tunde, Jiah, Nev and Kylie all began moving and speaking almost at once, as smoothly and seamlessly as a machine. Kylie **moved** her hand and a head-up display appeared in front of her, a portable hologram composed of squares, circles and triangles. Kylie smiled, nodded at a circle, and **suddenly** the ship was hovering three metres above the ground. It moved towards an **OPENING**. Kylie pressed the triangle with her mind. Another portal opened.

The ship eased through and the portal closed behind them.

And within seconds they were in deepest space. They whizzed ahead at hyper-ultra-mega speed. The conversation

they had was just like when they played the game.

'Surging ahead.'

'Stop saying surging! Doesn't make sense.'

'Moving ahead, then.'

'All right.'

'Super speed!'

'Hyper speed!'

'Ultra speed!'

Dembe was laughing. 'This is sick!'

'It's just like the game,' Tunde started to **explain**. 'I was meant to do this.'

Jiah interrupted, 'We're approaching the dimensional rip.'

And sure enough, there ahead of them were at least a hundred warships, sleek, white and hovering menacingly.

'There are too many of them. We have to destroy all of these ships,' **declared** the Supreme Leader.

'No,' Tunde said. 'We're not doing that.'

Aaven looked at him. 'You would dare speak to me like this? I'm your blood father. You do as I say.' He raised his claw, which was holding a stick. 'I am **holding** the talking stick, not you.'

Aan looked at him, gently prising the talking stick from his claws. 'What your father means, son, is your ideas are just as valid as ours. Your **ideas** are the new way. You are the Son Foreseen.'

Aaven spluttered. She looked at him. 'Well? Shall we let the boy lead on this or do you want to go the way you've always gone – war, war and more war – or peace?'

The Supreme Leader was tight-beaked and, after a moment, nodded in agreement. He retrieved the stick and said, 'All right, Son Foreseen. What would you suggest?'

Tunde looked at the others and said, 'The weapons on this ship don't just kill, remember. We **know** this stuff from the game. They can teleport. They can send things back in time, transport you light-years away so that you're no longer an immediate threat. We use those instead of the kill switch.'

As they approached the dimensional rip, several Furleenian ships came forward.

Juba put his head in his hands. 'This is Tnkaaah. He was **never happy** with peace. He would rather toy with the enemy, then rip them to shreds with his claws. He has no respect for the diplomatic process.'

Dembe looked at them. 'This guy's called *Tinker*? That's ridiculous.'

Suddenly there were blasts of fire coming at them from all sides, and the ship rocked. Kylie took aim and **fired back**, like the expert markswoman she was.

Tunde thought to himself, *Shields up*, and solid light-shields appeared all about the ship. They looked like strange waffles made of light, but each direct hit they took just bounced off. The ship was **SAFE**, intact and still flying.

'Phew,' muttered Tunde. 'This is a bit different from when we play at home.'

The Supreme Leader grunted his approval. 'Aviaan technology is far superior to Furleenian rubbish.'

Juba winced. Aaven saw, and held up his stick. 'With due

respect, I do not wish to cause offence.'

Juba nodded. 'Kylie's mother is truly a diplomatic genius,' he said.

Kylie beamed with pride.

Suddenly the ship shook again.

'I need to be out there,' Tunde insisted. 'We're sitting ducks.' He tapped his chest three times and his wings flew out from his back.

Dembe said, 'Did you say "duck"? You look more like an eagle and a swan had a baby.'

Suddenly a blaster and several switches appeared on Tunde's uniform.

Dembe slipped into his seat. 'We'll cover you,' she said. 'Be careful out there.'

Marcus leaped to his feet. 'Hang on,' he said, producing a gun. 'You are not leaving me behind. I have spent my whole life working away for that stuffy old man and his dreams of peace, and I am not going to miss out on an up close and personal real-life alien battle.'

Tunde looked at Marcus, who was brandishing his gun. 'No way – you're a liability,' he said, making a gesture with his hand. Everyone **watched** as Marcus was immediately secured by gelatinous bonds and the gun clattered to the ground.

'Sorted,' said Tunde. 'Now let's go make some peace.'

11

BATTLE STATIONS

'**W**e're taking the fight to them,' said Tunde. 'S.H.I.P.P.E., shields up. Jiah, Nev, Kylie, Dembe – it's your deck.'

And then he exited the spacecraft with his birth parents.

'OK, ladies, now let's get in formation!' Kylie yelled out. 'You too, Nev.'

Jiah laughed. She was loving working out directional shifts and battle strategy on her computer read-out, counting the Furleenian rogue attack ships and figuring out how to take them on.

Dembe looked at monitors all around the spacecraft and marvelled. She couldn't help admiring their poise in a battle situation.

'You're all so . . . **CALM**. Like things like this happen every day. We're all in spacesuits and there's a giant cat, two bird-people, and Tunde – *and* there's a whole heap of enemy spacecrafts and they wanna destroy us . . .'

Nev grinned and said, 'It was either this or physics revision – take your pick!'

Aaven, who had been listening through the communication mic, with mounting impatience, snapped:

'Do Earth younglings ever stop talking? We are in the battle time now – we demand your attention, not this inane prattle! Silence.'

Aan sighed into her mic. 'And you **wonder** why your subjects don't quite take to you when they meet you . . .'

Aaven whipped round to face her.

'What do you mean, they don't take to me? What have they been saying?'

Aan just **laughed**.

'I daren't say, you've still got the talking stick.'

He looked down at his gauntlets and saw that he was clutching the stick like a sergeant major. He handed it to her.

'Sorry. You take this for a while . . .'

'*Wait*,' said Kylie. 'The ships have gone. Look.'

They looked around. It was true.

'Why?' asked Tunde, now eyeing the **empty** space around him. 'Where have the ships gone?'

Aaven shrugged. 'They will return. This is called strategy. We must wait.'

Meanwhile, as Tunde floated, waiting for some sign of an attack, he scanned the skies and tried to conjure up a **description** that might do this startling vista some justice; the contrast between the inky blackness and brightness of the surrounding star-scape. He imagined himself encircled by an endless Afro with a diamond-encrusted crown on top. Eventually he gave up trying to think of what it looked like. Space was basically top-notch, innit?

He had to get used to it, though, or he'd be useless in the coming battle. Tunde spoke into his comms mic.

'When you see them we need to act fast. We're gonna teleport them a thousand light-years away. Worst case scenario, they'll go back in time and be furry babies – and we'll leave one or two others to get them back.'

Aaven grumbled in a **disgruntled fashion** and said: 'If that's the plan, that's the plan. But you are foolish. They wish to destroy the planet of your birth. This is kill or be killed.'

Tunde snapped back, 'We're not doing that. We don't do that.'

And then he heard what sounded like a cross between a high-pitched scream and a roar – **eeeeeeeeeeeee AWWWWWWRRRRRRRRRRRR!**

And not one, not two, not ten, but three hundred attack pods came at them in attack formation. Tunde panicked.

Jiah, Nev, Dembe and Kylie spoke almost as one.

'Assuming battle stations. All weapons on standby.'

And then, suddenly, Tunde heard a **FWOOOOOOOOSH-ING** sound behind him – it was Aaven and Aan in full Aviaan battle-warrior mode – wings extended, uniforms bristling with odd-looking tech. Neither of them looked like they were prepared to take any rubbish from anyone.

'If we die at this moment, we will die as warriors,' said Aaven.

Jiah sat in her space on S.H.I.P.P.E. Uncharacteristically, she was crying. 'I don't want to be a warrior, I want to go home.

The mathematical computations regarding our **survival** at this point are . . . put it this way: there will be no birthday party for me this year.'

Aan heard Jiah through her earpiece and said, 'S.H.I.P.P.E., perhaps something to calm Jiah right now.'

A boy-band ballad began to play in Jiah's earphones. She was a little happier and said, 'Ahh, I like this one. I still think I'm egg mayo on toast though . . .'

Aaven shook his head at this mollycoddling.

'Let us enter the fray – no more banter or music. Today we throw ourselves into the battle – the battle for peace, I mean.'

Aan flew directly towards the oncoming enemy horde, yelling: 'Beak and claw! **NO MORE TALK! LET THE BATTLE FOR PEACE BEGIN!**'

And as the two alien warriors began firing beams and blasts at various cat-shaped spacecraft, Tunde took a breath and spoke to his friends.

'Look, I don't know how this works, but Jiah, you and S.H.I.P.P.E. need to work out what's gonna damage these ships just enough, so that no one dies but they know we mean business, and they can high-tail it home. Everyone else, we need to aim to disable shields 'til they've worked it out – remember, **no killing**.'

At her console onboard S.H.I.P.P.E., Dembe bit her lip nervously. She alone had not played the game before.

Tunde flew in a lazy circle and pulse-blasted a Furleenian craft – it juddered away from him and then he turned a backflip and teleported it back in time.

Meanwhile Jiah and S.H.I.P.P.E. had produced a 3-D hologram version of what was going on outside. Dembe and Nev were shouting out instructions, and Kylie scanned her head-up display and made a mental note of where the enemy ships were. She flexed her fingers, took perfect aim and started firing.

Dembe's voice beamed into Tunde's ears. She was laughing.

'Juba's playing with a ball of string and Marcus Humphries is practically wetting himself cos he wants to see this. I can't say I blame him. I just wouldn't wanna miss any of this! I've wanted to do this my whole life. No way you're getting away with doing all this on your own.'

Tunde smiled. He was no longer scared – he knew (sort of) what he had to do –

'Snap grid of surrounding skyscape!'

As soon as he had said that, the largest ship came into view. It was the biggest object Tunde had ever seen in his life – a giant cat battle-cruiser was taking up almost the entire space-scape. **TUNDE GULPED**. This wasn't a game any more.

Almost on cue, the rogue leader of the Furleenians' voice **RANG** in their heads like an annoying bullhorn.

'*Pathetic creatures of this domain! It is I, Rogue Leader Tnkaaah of the Furleenian Revolutionary caucus. For you, this battle is over – we have you now. We also understand that the turncoat Juba resides with you . . . he will be dealt with accordingly.*'

Juba looked up and stopped playing with his ball of string at Tnkaaah's voice.

Tnkaaah continued:

'*And by "dealt with accordingly" I mean "stuffed in a sack and then tossed into the nearest sun". It is not your role in life to command us to sue for peace, Juba — that you would seek to parley with our sworn enemies speaks of cowardice, betrayal and treason! You will die for this in the most painful of ways for a Furleenian. Then we'll do the same with your new best friends and then everyone you know, everyone you love, your furlings, your elders . . .*'

Aaven sniffed. 'He'd never give up the talking stick, would he?'

Aan nodded in agreement. 'Never stops.'

Jiah laughed despite her fear. 'What a windbag!'

Tnkaaah continued:

'*We know you shield the Supreme Leader of the Aviaan. We will especially enjoy snuffing him out. And then we shall annihilate his entire family — especially this so-called Son Foreseen, who was going to bring about this namby-pamby, niminy-piminy period of eternal peace. PAH! I spit on your peace —*'

And suddenly the Furleenian command ship changed in **APPEARANCE** — at first it had been smooth and aerodynamic, now it presented itself in matt black attack mode — and it bristled with weapons, shields and white light, with massive cannons focused upon them and the Earth beyond.

'**YIKES**,' muttered Dembe.

Aaven turned to Tunde.

'*Time to be brave, or allow everyone you care about to disappear forever.*'

'Does the ship have any weak spots, Jiah?'

'Left paw, Tunde.'

Tunde found himself remembering something. When he'd played S.H.I.P.P.E. Space Fighter in solo mode, a logo would appear from time to time at the top right of the head-up display.

It was a small orange logo in the shape of a dragon-type bird-thing – to which only top-scoring players could gain access. He had played on that level repeatedly.

Tunde flew up front and hovered centrally in front of the command module, which resembled an enormous cat's head with two paws on the bottom left and right.

He closed his eyes momentarily and suddenly felt huge, powerful and suffused with an incredible energy source that was unstoppable.

As the command module fired its enormous blasters at the Earth, Tunde felt himself flying towards the blasts.

Dembe cried out as she watched – Tunde was flying towards enemy fire – and did he look bigger or something? Much bigger – he seemed to fill the entire horizon. Plus, he was GLOWING BRIGHTER and brighter . . . like a Tunde-shaped star.

The blasts hit him, but Tunde absorbed them.

Jiah was freaking.

'What's that? What's he doing? How is he doing that? This wasn't in the game!'

Nev agreed.

'I ain't never seen him do this before . . .'

Jiah was yelling.

'Look at him go, though – it's like he was meant to do this!'

Aaven spoke to all of them, his voice solemn.

'This is why he is the Son Foreseen. Once in an aeon, a hatchling is born with the power to level a domain. Tunde is a Dragonwing.'

The Furleenian command module **FIRED** more blasts at an alarming rate. Tunde felt himself surge with energy – he absorbed these attacks too – and at one point, he laughed, then said:

'Hello. My name's Tunde. I've just absorbed your worst firepower.'

The ship fired another massive wide beam of energy directly at him now – Tunde increased in size and swallowed the blast whole as if it were an enormous Chocolate Orange.

'As I was about to say – unless you want me to turn all the energy I've just absorbed back on to you – like this . . .'

And at this point, he burped, and a solid blast of flaming energy flew across space and incinerated the bottom-left paw of the ship. Explosive force leaped from the hits and the command module rocked back and forth.

Tunde continued, his voice loud and confident, a confidence that came from deep inside, for at last, this was who he was.

'My name is Tunde Wilkinson, and my friends and I don't

like bullies at all. Don't come back here – anybody who does will be dealt with like this –'

Tunde **burped** again and this time blue flame flew from his mouth and took out all the cannons atop the Furleenian command module. Tnkaaah was yelling –

'*Retreat! We must go back! This is bad, very bad. We should never have done this – never. Retreeaaat!*'

And just like that the rogue command leader, his ship and his remaining attack pods were gone. Tunde, the Dragonwing, and his best friends had saved the day.

Tunde flew towards them in full majestic Dragonwing mode – a beautiful, almost dinosaur-like version of an enormous light-filled bird-creature of myth.

As he approached the rip in space through which the Furleenian rogue force had **FLOWN**, Tunde focused upon it with all his energies. There was something he had to do.

He opened his mouth and a pitch-black flame flew from his lips, and, in an explosion of anti-light, welded the rip shut. He made short work of it, even though the tear in space was thousands of miles high and wide; with every single iota of **energy** in his body, he blasted this fatal tear in space until it was gone.

And then suddenly – VOOMF! – an implosion of black light, and Tunde was back to winged mode. His uniform was a little singed, his wings folded, and he was floating in mid-space. Aan glided towards him – caught and held him in her arms.

'*Let's get you back to the ship.*'

12

BACK ON BOARD S.H.I.P.P.E.

They materialized back on board. And then it was celebration time. Nev put on his **BANGING** mix tape of choons and then immediately busted some moves, which he found difficult in his new spacesuit. He gave up after a while during a particularly embarrassing attempt at a head-spin that ended with him bouncing off a control panel.

Dembe held her hands in front of her face.

Jiah said, '**Breakdancing** in space – where's the sense in that?'

Kylie just grinned. 'The Nevmeister's got the funk.'

Tunde was happy too.

'Good, good, we're all happy. Let's go home. I'm starving.'

They all **jumped** in then.

'What's the best celebration food?'

'Pizza.'

'Jerk chicken, rice, peas and dumplings.'

'**Vegetarian biryani**.'

'McNuggets.'

'Multi-level-heart-stopper-whoppa-burger.'

'AND CHIPS!'

'That is sick.'

'That's like barf-a-rama-ville man!'

Marcus Humphries couldn't stand it any more. No one had noticed that his hands were free; he stood up, snatched a nearby pulse blaster from S.H.I.P.P.E.'s wall and started waving it around.

'That's right! I am free! It appears your ship can only multi-task up to a certain point. Once you were all celebrating **BLOWING UP** the big bad pussycat monsters, I armed myself with this little beauty.'

Tunde staggered to his feet, weak from his Dragonwing exertions. His wings were folded away and he didn't look like the Son Foreseen any more – he just **looked** like plain old Tunde.

'Please, Mr Humphries – we should go back home. We need to finish what we started, get peace sorted between the Furleenians and the Aviaans. And I – I've gotta talk to my parents: we've got a lot to talk about.'

Marcus **laughed** incredulously.

'Home? Back to Earth? This minute? Oh no no no no no no no no no no! I want to see where the birdy duo and ginger-face come from. We need to go there, blow a few more of them away and then take as much of their tech as possible back to The Facility. Then once we've figured out how it all works we'll sell all the ideas and be **BILLIONAIRES!**'

He looked at them as if they were stupid. He kept pointing the blaster at them.

Tunde said, 'Not interested.'

Kylie said, 'Me neither.'

Nev said, 'Bruv, put the fing down, man.'

Juba said, 'Our technology, as you call it, is aeons old. Only we **understand** how it truly works. You'll never, in a billion ages, be able to decipher their inner workings.'

Marcus said, 'Well, if I may be so bold, I *am* one of the cleverest people on Earth. I'm the one who sussed out the relationship between Aviaan DNA and how to control this ship. I worked out that we needed Tunde to fl𝖞 it. I did all that myself! I tried to get Tunde's adopted father on the project, but he was useless. In the end, if you want something doing, you have to do it yourself. You can't rely on the help.'

Tunde bristled. 'The help?' he said quietly.

Marcus waved the blaster around. 'He was absolutely useless. I guess your Mum's the smarter one! Come on then. Let's go.'

Tunde shook his head and said, 'S.H.I.P.P.E., light-bar cage, please – Humphries, Marcus.'

And bars of light shot out of the hull, surrounding Humphries, knocking the blaster from his hand, completely encasing him.

Tunde spoke coldly.

'My mum's a genius. She's the one who understood what S.H.I.P.P.E. could do and she let us **discover how to work** it out ourselves, with no help from anyone else. She deserves a better boss than you.'

Marcus was becoming scared – the light bars were moving whichever way he went.

'Look, I didn't mean that about your mum and dad – he's quite clever actually – all that gene splicing, messing around with vegetables and fruit and fish and things. Very clever. If you like that kind of thing.'

In a very CALM, matter-of-fact voice, Tunde said, 'Mr Humphries – it's over. I want to go to school. Take my exams. Be with my friends. I just want to be normal.'

He looked at Aaven and Aan, and smiled ruefully.

Marcus gave a little shriek of frustration.

'You've got no ambition. I agree with Aaven, you should've killed them all. We could be rich!'

'You're wrong, Mr Humphries. And maybe you'd know that if you'd been raised by amazing parents, like mine. All that stuff matters.' Tunde GLANCED at his devol blaster. 'You have to go back.'

And in his mind he spoke to S.H.I.P.P.E. directly:

'Humphries, Marcus – devol – hatchling status in three, two, one . . .'

The devol blast enveloped Marcus. The light bars expanded so everyone could see what was *happening* to him.

Marcus was reversing in age! The forty-something male **human scientist** trapped behind the light bars became thirty years old, then twenty and whisked through ten, five, four, and then – abruptly – and slightly pulsing at that, there was a large egg on the floor of the ship. Tunde picked it up, walked carefully to a control panel, looked at it and it opened. Two doors slid back and he **placed** the egg within, and then closed it again with a thought.

Tunde looked at everybody. No one challenged him or said he was wrong; no one looked disappointed with him. He had done the right thing.

Nev said, 'Good riddance.'

Dembe said, 'I was gonna hit him upside the head with the fire extinguisher but you had it all under control, T.'

Jiah grinned and said, 'I wonder how many points you'll get for getting rid of him? You know, in the game. I bet if we did a survey of everyone in his life, including his parents, friends and family – no one would be that fussed about not seeing his ugly mush again.'

'Come on,' said Kylie. 'Let's go home. My mum always goes to a great place for an Indian head massage. They have a hot tub and everything. I think after we just saved the entire world, we deserve a spa day, don't we?'

Tunde FWOOOSHED out his wings.

'Spa day! Spa day! Spa day! SPA DAY!'

And with everyone chanting like this (even the Aviaan and Furleenian contingent who had no idea what a spa day actually was), S.H.I.P.P.E. entered stealth mode and steered a course back to The Facility.

13

ENDS AND NEW BEGINNINGS

The magpie and several thousand friends, family, close relations and hangers-on occupied the trees which overlooked The Facility. They **cooed and cawed** and screeched and squawked as vehicles drove in and out of the building. The birds screeched noisily, jumped up and down and flapped their wings in sequence, and for a moment it looked like a joyous feathery Mexican wave. The bird-boy had returned from beyond in triumph.

Back in the sub-sub-subterranean landing bay, S.H.I.P.P.E.'s mostly pre-teen crew, led by Tunde, **disembarked** from the craft.

Emil Krauss gave a sigh of relief and ran to meet everyone; Tunde was holding something rather carefully, and when the professor was finally close enough, he was handed a large, creamy, glowing egg.

'What is this?' asked Krauss.

'Erm. This is Marcus Humphries,' Tunde said. 'We devolved him – he's an embryo right now, waiting for the right moment to be hatched.'

'It's all right, Tunde. You had to do what you had to do, his intentions were never that honourable. We'll raise him right this time and make sure he has a mum and dad like yours.'

Ruth and Ron flung their arms around Tunde.

Suddenly they were surrounded by his **FRIENDS** who all wanted to talk excitedly about the part they'd played in repelling the enemy.

'We flew that mission perfectly,' said Kylie. 'Saw danger from every conceivable angle.'

'I worked those angles out myself,' Jiah boasted. 'In my head and on the back of a tissue whilst also co-piloting and keeping control of my bladder, which was tough due to the fact that I'd NEVER BEEN IN SPACE BEFORE!'

Dembe was listening and nodding quietly – she was humbled by the whole experience. They'd just fought a battle IN SPACE!

Nev just shook his head and said, 'We had your back out there, cuz. No thanks necessary.'

'You were brave too, Nev,' Tunde said. 'We just saved everyone on Earth from an alien attack!'

'Yeah,' said Nev. 'That's weird.'

Dembe **PATTED** Tunde on the shoulder. 'Congratulations, T,' she said at last. 'You sent them angry cats packing.'

Tunde bit his lip. 'Did I do the right thing though? I couldn't kill them. I just hope I didn't let my mates down. Or my mum and dad.'

Dembe looked at him in surprise.

'This lot? Are you kidding?' She nodded at Kylie and Jiah

and Nev, at Ruth and Ron, and Aan and Aaven. 'They love you – all of them. Even when you were in nuclear Dragonwing mode. That was awesome, by the way . . . But seriously. You didn't need to do any more than what you did today – which was be yourself. Look at them. You've got all the people who love you right here. Your parents love you and want the best for you. Be happy with that. I've been fostered all my life – no one has ever cared about me that way . . .'

Before she could **finish**, Tunde hugged her as tight as he'd ever hugged anyone. 'Thank you,' he whispered.

Dembe burst into tears. 'Now look what's happened,' she said furiously. 'You're gonna make me look bad in front of the bird-people. **Get off!**'

He let her go and stood to one side as she wiped her eyes.

So much had happened in just one day. The Dragonwing had changed Tunde forever. And there were a few **changes** he wanted to make.

In the planning room back at The Facility, he faced both his birth parents and said:

'I think you both need to do some more work on yourselves before you're gonna be great leaders. From now on, I advise you to take on everything Kylie's mum tells you – you can't just **SAY** you're gonna change and not do it. And listen to Juba. He's a really good advisor. You've got to be more about protecting and serving the Aviaan rather than just attacking anybody who steps on your toes at the pub.'

Aaven – who had no idea what a pub was – nodded respectfully. 'You are right, Dragonwing,' he murmured. 'War shall become peace.' And he and Aan smiled at each other.

Later, Krauss had everyone sit round the table: Ron, Ruth, Tunde, Aan, Aaven, Juba, Kylie, Jiah, Dembe and Nev.

He cleared his throat. 'I've just had a Zoom call with all the world leaders who have been **SUPPORTING** our work. They all agree that we owe you kids a great deal of gratitude. Your futures are taken care of. And if there is anything you need, tell me and I will make it happen.'

'Now that you mention it, I need a few things,' said Nev. 'I want to play for Man City one day – but more than that, I want to be Tunde's friend and help him do whatever he can to protect everyone.'

Krauss nodded. 'Worthy aims,' he murmured. 'I think that could be arranged.'

'I want to fly S.H.I.P.P.E. again. And protect Tunde, of course,' said Kylie.

'I want a job at The Facility,' said Jiah, her eyes shining.

'You would be a true asset,' said Krauss.

Kylie turned to Tunde. 'What about you? Now you've saved the world, what would you like to happen?'

Tunde looked over to where Ron and Ruth were sitting. He didn't have to think too hard. To his credit, the boy with wings kept it very simple.

'I want to stay with my mum and dad. I wouldn't be here without them.'

They all looked at Dembe, who shrugged sadly. 'I just want better foster parents – people who don't bully me or make me change the way I wear my clothes and hair. Of course, going into space is fun, but I want more.'

Tunde turned and whispered in Ruth's ear. Ruth turned to Ron and whispered in his ear, and then he turned to Krauss and whispered in his ear.

Krauss laughed. 'That would certainly be a solution,' he said. 'We'll have to go through the appropriate channels, but I see no reason why not.'

Ruth turned to Dembe. 'If we can make it work, and you'd like to,' she said, 'we'd like you to live with us. We could adopt you properly.'

'I warn you, they can't cook,' Tunde said, grinning. 'But they're all right really. Better than all right.'

Dembe practically did a cartwheel across the room, but then stopped herself and looked at Ron and Ruth carefully.

'My hair stays the same,' she said firmly. 'As do my clothes. I only eat certain things. I listen to weird music. And I've got Tunde's back at school. Cool?'

Ron and Ruth nodded joyously. They'd always wanted another child.

Professor Krauss cleared his throat. 'I'm afraid there is one last thing I have to tell you. There could be more inter-dimensional and intergalactic rips and you're the only one who could do something about it. I can give you access to whatever resources you need to make better lives for **YOURSELVES**, because you are all now Earth's most powerful secret weapon.'

Nev laughed.

Kylie hiccupped.

Jiah looked at Tunde.

Dembe had a big smile on her face.

Tunde was so happy he could almost burst.

And so began the next phase of the adventure.

And that's exactly what happened. Everybody benefited from their new status. Ron Wilkinson was at last promoted and very **happily** continued to work on an organic bungalow-sized blueberry. On top of that, he was also given the role as Krauss's chief advisor and friend. 'I'll keep The Facility on the straight and narrow.'

Ruth was in charge of learning everything possible about Aviaan tech and honing it so that Tunde, Dembe, Nev, Jiah and Kylie could operate everything in a more efficient way.

Dembe **MOVED** in with the Wilkinsons and became the troubled pre-teen daughter they'd always wanted. She and Tunde were now **best friends** and battle companions.

The gang played S.H.I.P.P.E. Space Fighter every day and Ruth's changes in the operating system were brilliant. The ship still spoke to them, which was fine except when it said things like, 'Keep your display tidy' and 'Make sure you go for a wee before you take me out there', which got a bit weird. But still. No one seemed to mind.

There was one more difficult conversation Tunde had to have.

Aaven, Aan and Juba still wanted him to return to the Aviaan planet to **CONTINUE** work on the peace process. It was his duty, they said. On the day they were about to leave, Tunde told them that perhaps it was his duty to stay on Earth and live as normal a life as possible – *take* his exams, play football, go to university. He wanted to do everything his friends were doing.

'And so, you see,' he finished, 'I will do my duty – if Earth is ever under attack again, me and my mates will be there. But I *want* to have a normal life too.'

His parents and their diplomatic advisor nodded solemnly.

'You are wise, hatchling,' said Aaven.

Aan smiled. 'Earth agrees with you,' she said.

They returned to Aviaan in Aan's escape pod and vowed to stay in touch whenever they were **NEEDED**. Tunde agreed to contact them once a week via inter-dimensional Zoom.

Which left Ron and Ruth as his guardians. Their only task was to keep loving him, cooking him weird meals, and talking to him about life, love and the art of doing the right thing.

They had **evidence** from the Aviaan that the dimensional rip was holding, but there were other ways into Earth space and they were to remain watchful. But Krauss had no fear – with Tunde's powers and his back-up team, they had an unbeatable combination. Whenever and wherever the new threat came from, the team would be there. He just had to make doubly sure they knew what they were letting themselves in for.

One day Krauss summoned them to The Facility where they were given a fancy lunch and donned their uniforms and upgraded control panels for the ship. Also (and how cool is this!) the wingless among them were given Facility-made rocket-packs. And a name, which Tunde had chosen, although he hadn't told the others yet: Project Blackfire.

Tunde **cleared his throat** and began his speech.

'My friends, Kylie, Jiah, Nev, Dembe – you've made school bearable, but also you had my back at possibly the worst time of my life, and we're here. We **survived**. And now I'm proud to say that we're going to be Project Blackfire . . .'

Everybody clapped at this point.

Nev yelled, 'Yes, bruv!'

Jiah couldn't help herself.

'Technically we should be Team Dragonwing,' she said, 'but you're the captain so you choose – Team Blackfire is fine by me – just letting you know that technically—'

Kylie elbowed her in the ribs. 'Jiah, you're killing the vibe. Put a sock in it. Go on, Tunde.'

Tunde smiled. 'I just want to say thanks to everyone at The Facility for making all this possible. I know this all started out as an exploration and then they got more than they bargained for. I wouldn't be here if you lot weren't so **NOSEY**. Thank you, Professor Krauss.'

And he sat down. Ron and Ruth beamed at him, radiating pride for their boy. And he was their boy – Aaven and Aan may have been his birth parents, but as far as they were concerned, Tunde was theirs and theirs alone.

Professor Krauss stood up.

'Thank you, Tunde. I have one more thing to say. Your lives are about to *change*. This is the new normal. You will be on call twenty-four hours a day. I hope it won't come to that but it may, if the Earth is in severe danger. We are now tasked, for as long as it is needed, to protect the Earth and promote peace because it is the **right thing to do**.' Professor Krauss looked at them proudly.

'And what you should know is that in future, if anything out there threatens our way of life, or wants to destroy us, you should be proud to know that someone somewhere will be saying: "It's OK, Tunde and Project Blackfire will protect us."'

They all nodded solemnly and then The Facility drove them back to Tunde's house.

'When we get back I want to show them the you-know-what,' Tunde said.

Ruth **GRINNED**. 'All right,' she said. 'As it's a special day.'

'Come on,' Tunde said to his friends. 'There's a surprise.'

Tunde opened up the door to his **ROOM**. It had been reconfigured to contain a television screen that took up an entire wall. There was a long daybed and a couple of chairs

facing the TV, and a table in front of that – and **sitting** there were brand-new wrist-band controls and a console for the game – this was S.H.I.P.P.E.'s brand-new operating system. Each set of controls came with 3-D goggles. Everyone cheered, sat down and prepared themselves. Ruth stood by the door and watched them as they got ready to play. Ron appeared behind her and looked at them all.

'I hope Tunde doesn't think that being an inter-dimensional space fighter means he can **slack off** with his homework.'

Ruth smiled.

'They're not just playing at saving the world any more. They'll need as many practice runs as possible.'

Ron **nodded**, and together they went downstairs, leaving the kids playing furiously.

'Funny old world, isn't it?' said Ron.

'I know,' said Ruth. 'Good job Tunde and his mates are here to keep it safe.'

Then they went into the kitchen **to make** who-knows-what sandwiches and 'Oh my gosh, that tastes weird' drinks for everyone.

And the magpie watched from the window ledge and was pleased. The boy had done it and he was home again. All was well.

THE DRAGONWING AFTERMATH

Story: Lenny Henry
Art: Mark Buckingham
Letters: Todd Klein

RON AND RUTH AND TUNDE AND DEMBE NOW LIVE TOGETHER IN THE FARMHOUSE BY THE BUS STOP.

TUNDE AND DEMBE BEHAVE JUST LIKE BROTHER AND SISTER: IT'S AS THOUGH THEY WERE HATCHED FROM THE SAME EGG.

THE REST OF THE GANG WERE THERE ALL THE TIME TOO, TO EAT SNACKS, DRINK SODA POP, AND PLAY "LET'S DEFEND THE EARTH" VIA S.H.I.P.P.E.'S COMPUTER PROGRAMS.

OF COURSE, THEY WERE STILL ON HAND TO HELP AT THE FACILITY.

KRAUSS, RON AND RUTH TALK STRATEGY.

ALL LINKS WITH THE BIRTH PARENTS WERE KEPT OPEN.

AND JUBA, OF COURSE.

MEANWHILE, NEV HAS ENDEARED HIMSELF TO AAVEN AND AAN BY RECOMMENDING VARIOUS SONGS FROM HIS PLAYLIST THAT THEY MIGHT LIKE:

YEAH, YOU NEED SOME LIKE...

...MARSHMELLO, YEAH, SOME PROTOJE-- LIKE, TYLA YAWEH, SOME LIL MOSEY'S BANGIN'.

HE CAME FOR MY MUM AND DAD. WE SHOULD NEVER HAVE LET HIM GO THE LAST TIME.

WE'VE GOT YOUR BACK, BRUV.

TNKAAAH'S VOICE CAME OUT OF THE MONITORS FOR ALL OF THEM TO HEAR.

ONCE I'M DONE WITH YOU, I'M **DESTROYING** EVERYTHING ON YOUR PLANET AND I'LL KEEP WHATEVER'S LEFT AS A PLAYTHING.

AND HE LAUGHS.

OPEN THE DOOR, S.H.I.P.P.E.

AS HE FLEW TOWARDS THE SHIP, HIS MIND A BLUR OF ANGER AND HATRED AND FEAR....

...HE WANTED TO DESTROY THE FURLEENIAN SHIP AND EVERYONE IN IT.

BUT JUST THEN HE THOUGHT OF WHAT HIS MUM AND DAD MIGHT SAY.

ALL THE LESSONS HE'D BEEN TAUGHT ABOUT PEOPLE WHO LOOKED LIKE HIM WHO HAD CHANGED THINGS BY PROTEST AND NEGOTIATION AND THEIR WITS.

TNKAAAH AND THE SHIP IMMEDIATELY VANISHED...

...AND REAPPEARED.

POP!

WHAT DO WE HAVE HERE?

Acknowledgements

Just as Tunde couldn't have saved the world without his friends and allies, a book doesn't come together without the help of a whole group of people. Thank you to my editorial team, including Sam Smith, Krystle Appiah, Genevieve Herr and Amy Boxshall, my readers Kieran Fanning, Jen Campbell, Laura Henry-Allain, Sarah Shaffi and the help of Belinda Sherlock, Sam Amidon and Ellie Humphries.

Thank you as well to my brilliant agent, Natalie Jerome (and her daughter, beta reader Talah). To the illustrators Keenon Ferrell and Mark Buckingham for bringing my characters to life on the page. Thank you to the Macmillan team for getting this brilliant book into YOUR hands including Alison Ruane, Anthony Forbes Watson, Becky Lloyd, Belinda Ioni Rasmussen, Lara Borlenghi, Laura Carter, Michele Young, Sarah Clarke, Rachel Graves, Rachel Vale and Tom Cookson.

And, of course, to Lisa and Esme.

About the Illustrators

Keenon Ferrell is an illustrator and animator based in New York. He makes artwork inspired by music, fashion and sports. He also has a love for storytelling, fantasy and history which can be seen throughout his work. Keenon's clients include: Netflix, Capital One, StoryCorps and Sony Music Entertainment, to name a few.

Mark Buckingham has been creating comics for thirty-five years, building a reputation for design, storytelling and a chameleon-like diversity of art styles. He is best known as the regular artist on Bill Willingham's multiple-award-winning Fables series and for his work with Neil Gaiman on *Miracleman*, *Sandman* and *Death*. He previously collaborated with Lenny Henry on his memoir *Who Am I, Again?*